The Ice Boy

Patricia Elliott

Hodder
Children's
Books

A division of Hodder Headline Limited

Copyright © 2002 Patricia Elliott
First published in Great Britain in 2002
by Hodder Children's Books

The right of Patricia Elliott to be identified as the author of
this Work has been asserted by her in accordance with the
Copyright, Designs and Patents Act 1988.

3

A Catalogue record for this book is available
from the British Library

ISBN 0 340 85424 3

Typeset by Avon Dataset Ltd, Bidford-on-Avon, Warks

Printed and bound in Great Britain by
Clays Ltd, St Ives plc

The paper and board used in this paperback by
Hodder Children's Books are natural recyclable products
made from wood grown in sustainable forests.
The manufacturing processes conform to the environmental
regulations of the country of origin.

Hodder Children's Books
A division of Hodder Headline Limited
338 Euston Road
London NW1 3BH

In memory of my father

Acknowledgements

With heartfelt thanks to my friends Gill and Ruth
without whose persistent nagging I would
never have entered for the Fidler Award.

CHAPTER ONE

Show No One

It had been a mistake for him and Matt to come back, Edward thought, as he trudged along the top of the sea wall.

If their uncle hadn't wanted them to come to him for their usual summer holiday, hadn't almost insisted on it to Mum, they could have stayed in London and kept all the memories shut safely away. It was only their first afternoon back at Uffenham, but already he kept expecting to see Dad everywhere.

His older brother Matt was some way behind him on the sea wall, hidden by parked cars. The wall was as broad as a road. People drove on to it up an earth slope, then parked on the top to gaze out over the cold waves of the North Sea. There was an empty old Martello tower at the far end. On previous holidays Matt and Edward had often tried to climb through its high windows, but had never succeeded.

Today, force of habit had somehow drawn their feet in that direction. But Matt had been silent as they started off along the wall, lost in his own thoughts; not looking down at the shingle beach and the sea, or over to the other side of the wall where the river curled away from the sailing club through the marshes, but just frowning down at his trainers.

'Matt? Come on! Matt!'

Edward's shout was sucked away by the wind. Below him, where the shingle became sand at the sea's edge, a small boy, watched over by his father, dug with a yellow plastic spade. The shingle gleamed alabaster and mother-of-pearl and the waves creamed against the breakwaters. The waves were small today, well-behaved and tidy. They knew their place. They drew back respectfully before they reached up too far. Not like the day last summer when Dad had—

Edward's eyes stung with the wind. It was cold on top of the wall. He shoved his hands further into his jacket pockets. He'd go on to the tower on his own for something to do, then he'd go back to his uncle's cottage, to Fen's cheerful chat and comforting slices of rather stale cake. He'd forget about Matt and his moods.

The Martello tower was squat and dark against the pale summer sky, rising up from a shingle hollow. From a distance, half its height was hidden. The ground sloped up from the riverbank, towards the edge of the hollow so that it looked as if it grew from a grassy mound, like a vast tree-stump. The mound was covered in lumps of sugary-white concrete, left over from the building of the sea wall. As Edward drew closer he suddenly noticed that there was a man sitting on one of these rocks at the top of the mound, gazing out to sea.

Edward slowed down, then stopped altogether, rooted to the spot, staring at the man's back. He was too far off to see clearly, but he'd recognize that faded denim jacket anywhere, the particular way it creased and strained round the broad shoulders; he knew how it would smell of sun and salt. The man was wearing a hat. Underneath it, the hair would be fair, starting to thin slightly.

Edward began to tremble. Hope flooded him so that it was like a pain pushing against the bones of his chest.

'Dad?' he whispered. His lips stuck together. 'Dad?'

Then all at once horror gripped him in the bright sunlight. Dad was dead, wasn't he? If the figure turned its face to Edward, what would he see?

He turned and began to stumble away. He willed his legs to move under him, to get him back along the sea wall. He'd got them running somehow when he saw Matt coming towards him, Matt looking up from his feet at last and staring at him.

'Where are you off to so fast?'

Edward sank down on a concrete bollard and gripped his hands together. Matt, suddenly concerned, bent over him. 'What's up? You look terrible.'

He put his hand to his mouth to stop his teeth chattering. 'I've just seen Dad!'

For a moment Matt looked shaken. 'What do you mean? It can't possibly be Dad.'

'It was!' Edward's fingers trembled against his mouth.

Matt stared at him. 'Hey, calm down.'

'But we've got to hurry!'

'Look, Ed, it's only someone who looks like him.'

'They never found him. There was just the boat . . . We don't *know* anything. We never have. Come on, Matt, please!'

'Oh, OK,' Matt said wearily. 'Anything to shut you up.'

They set off along the wall again. Edward's legs still felt weak but it was always difficult to co-ordinate them these days. They were growing too fast for the rest of him. Matt, taller and faster, loped ahead, his face closed, set against the wind.

The man was still sitting there, solid and real, facing away from them.

'That's not Dad!' hissed Matt.

'Yes, it is!'

'Shout to him, then. Call him. Go on!'

Edward bit his lip. 'I can't.'

They both crept stealthily, almost guiltily, nearer the man, until they were on the slope of the mound. They were so close now they could hear him sigh as he stared out over the small movement of the waves, so close they could almost feel the fierce and robust life vibrating from his broad bulk. They ducked down behind a lump of concrete.

'This is totally embarrassing,' whispered Matt angrily.

'He's wearing Dad's jacket.'

'Loads of people wear denim jackets. And Dad never wore hats!'

A pang of doubt went through Edward. The hat was a straw boater, battered but still recognizably a boater, like those that people who pretended to be artists wore, when they came up to East Anglia for painting courses in the summer. Dad had always joked about them.

Suddenly, taking them both by surprise, the man stood up in one swift movement and turned. Edward was so startled his knees gave way under him as he crouched there, and he fell sideways on to the grass. Beside him, Matt unbent his long legs and stood up awkwardly. Edward didn't look at him. Hope had drained away from him so fast he felt he was losing his life's blood. He wanted to weep with disappointment.

The man's face was nothing like Dad's.

Under the broad brim of the hat the man wore an eye patch. The other eye stared at them: an unwinking blue glare in his brown, lined face. He was old, and the surface of his face was so scored with tiny lines it was like the bark of an oak tree. In spite of his age he seemed to Edward, still lying sprawled on the ground, to be as tall and upright as a tree as well. He made Matt look small and insignificant.

'Now look what you've got us into!' Matt hissed.

He dragged Edward up and began stammering an apology to the old man, who continued to stand there silent and impassive. Eventually Matt gave up, his face scarlet, and blundered off down the mound, ignoring Edward's agonized expression.

The last thing Edward wanted was to be left alone with the old man, yet he couldn't bring his limbs to move. It was as if his body still refused to believe what his eyes had accepted. But at last embarrassment jerked him into life. He turned to go after Matt.

'No. You. Stop!'

The command rang out, bouncing off the bricks of the tower: deep, guttural-sounding, expecting instant obedience. It was directed at Edward, and his ears rang with it. The blue eye shone at him unnervingly. The man even raised a leathery hand. There was nothing for it but to obey.

He was beckoning to him now. Edward stayed where he was. The old man was obviously immensely strong and looked sinister with his eye patch. Except for a lone figure coming along the beach below, there was no one within shouting distance. Edward felt danger pass like a breath, over the top of his head.

'Come closer.' The gesture was impatient. 'Come. I ask for your help.'

'*My* help?' Edward hesitated, then took a step forward reluctantly, trying not to imagine what was behind the eye patch.

'Yes, yes, you. It is you I want.'

The man's speech was hard to understand. He frowned past Edward at the walking figure below, as if worried about being interrupted. 'I want you to take a message. It is for my son.' He pulled a crumpled piece of paper from one of the pockets of his denim jacket. 'I write it now.'

'You want me to give that to your son?' asked Edward, bewildered.

The man nodded, with a curt dip of his head. 'My own time here is done.' He pulled a pencil stub from the same pocket, smoothed the paper out and scribbled rapidly, resting the paper on a rock.

Edward watched in consternation. 'But how do I find your son? What's his name?'

'He will know you. Here.' The man thrust the

paper out, and Edward took it dumbly. There was only one word on it, scrawled untidily and quite illegibly over its creased surface.

'Remind him,' said the man urgently. 'It is the word. It will save him in the end. There are those who want to know it. Show no one until you give it to my son. You understand?'

'But—' Edward began. The single eye blazed at him. He spread his hands. 'Yes, OK.'

The old man was looking down again at the walker, who had drawn closer. A strange look passed over his fierce features; his vitality seemed suddenly dulled. 'He comes,' he said softly. 'And you must go.'

The next moment, Edward, clutching the scrap of paper, was pushed violently backwards. He found himself sliding down the slope, away from the tower, and when he picked himself up, the walker had already climbed the beach steps and was striding along the sea wall towards the mound, the sunlight glinting on his hair. A man, out of place in a city suit: a dark streak that moved swiftly over the white rocks as he began to climb up towards the old man. In a minute they would meet.

Edward crammed the paper into the pocket of his jacket and waited a moment, watching, frowning into the sun. If the old man already knew the walker, why had he given Edward, a complete stranger, the message to deliver? Was the walker one of the people he didn't want to see it?

The figures were very black against the light. The old man was taller and broader than the walker, but he seemed to fall back as the other man approached. Now they were talking, arguing, their voices raised but inaudible.

Suddenly the walker shouted something, raised an arm against the sky.

Edward turned and began to run, leaving the stones behind, his trainers thudding on the hard-baked mud between the wall and the flat curve of the riverbank, where the boats of the sailing club lay on their trailers. There were no footsteps in pursuit. By the time he had reached the first boats beached on the rough grass, he was ashamed of his fear. Panting, he stopped and looked back.

The two figures had vanished. The rock-strewn mound was empty, the tower's dark silhouette smooth and undisturbed.

Edward thought of the raised hand, threatening, murderous even, black against the light sky. Could the walker have *pushed* the old man down into the shingle pit? But he'd heard nothing, no cry for help. What should he do? He was tempted to run on back to the safety of Uffenham and his uncle's cottage, yet intrigued. Where had the men gone?

Minutes passed. No one reappeared. Cautiously,

Edward retraced his steps up the mound until he was standing in the shadow of a large concrete rock and could look down. The tower rose bare and intimidating from its dry moat. There was no sign of the men down there; and no figures against the sun on the far side of the mound.

Beyond the tower, the sea rolled quietly and unceasingly against the long shingle spit that separated it from the river. Weeds and sea thistles had seeded themselves amongst the stones, but it was a desolate windswept place to venture along. You'd walk and walk until you were up to your neck in water. Edward knew the two men couldn't have done that.

But unless they had managed to climb into the tower, past the tangle of barbed wire that covered the bridge to the entrance, they had disappeared as completely as if they had both been borne away on the waves.

CHAPTER TWO

Dark Thoughts

Edward went down the mound on to the wall, then down the steps to the beach, and began to jog back to Uffenham along the edge of the sea, where the shingle had been washed away leaving bands of firm, dark-yellow sand. As he ran he could feel the paper with its one-word message scratching against the lining of his jacket pocket.

There were footprints on the sand, under his trainers, the deeply cut prints of heavy city shoes, and they were filling with sea water. He was following the walker's trail, only backwards.

Forget him, Edward thought. *I've got Matt to face when I get back.*

The thought of Matt slowed him down. Matt was certain to be in one of his moods when he arrived back at Gull Cottage. Matt always seemed so angry these days, impossible to talk to. And yet once they'd been so close. What had happened?

Dad.

There was ice in Edward's heart. He shivered. The wind was rising, buffeting him, bullying the clouds into a dark canopy. A fine drizzle blew about the beach in sheets.

He pulled his collar up. Down by his feet he could see a pale grey stone with freckles lying in the ribbon of smaller stones and shells left by the tide. He'd always collected stones. In the old days. But it was a pity to leave it there – just in case he decided to make a collection after all this summer.

He picked it up and put it in one of the pockets of his tracksuit bottoms. Soon he'd found several more. A long green stone, thin and flat, lying almost in the walker's footprints, caught his eye and he stowed it away to join the others. Then, feeling oddly comforted by the weight of stones on each side of him, he went on down the empty beach.

'You smell of sea and rain,' said Fen. 'Matt's upstairs, unpacking. Your uncle's gone to some auction and won't be back till supper.'

She was sitting at the kitchen table in her smock, working on a watercolour of a flowering plant. A length of striped cloth was tied in a turban round her head and below it her bright eyes glared at the plant sticking meekly out of a jar on the table

12

beside her. Edward, impressed with the turban, thought she looked like a particularly unpredictable and dangerous sultan. He took off his damp jacket and draped it over the back of a chair.

'Is that a rose?' he asked, seeing the pink petals.

'*Althaea officinalis*,' declared Fen. 'Or marsh mallow when it's being less grand. You've seen it around.'

'I have?' He peered over her shoulder at the delicate work on her pad.

Fen sold her wild flower paintings extremely successfully to the local shops, to be bought by holidaymakers. Now and then, when she had had enough of Uffenham and Uncle Hodder, she would take off round the world to paint more exotic species, then she'd reappear suddenly some months later, tanned to mahogany, with her eyes sharper and shinier than ever. She lived next door to Uncle Hodder, but over the years she'd come to spend most of her Uffenham time in Gull Cottage. Edward liked this arrangement as much as his uncle did. Fen was one of the best people he'd met, even if she couldn't cook. He'd grown up thinking of her as a real aunt.

Fen pushed the plant painting away. She sighed, leaning back in the kitchen chair to look at Edward and shooting out her legs in their baggy, rust-coloured trousers. He could see her toes, adorned with chipped gold nail varnish, poking out of her sandals.

'I hope you're still painting?' she said.

'Not much.'

'That's a pity. Any reason?'

'Too busy.' The gang would think painting was sad. They'd think collecting stones was sad, too. 'I met this weird old bloke on the beach just now,' Edward said quickly, before Fen pried any further. 'Did Matt tell you?' He bit his lip, wondering what Matt would have said.

She shook her head and looked at him enquiringly.

'He gave me a message to give his son, but he never told me his name!'

'His own name, or his son's?'

'Neither of them.'

She gave a quick bark of laughter. 'That's not much good, then, is it? What did he look like, this strange man?'

'He wore an eye patch. He was difficult to understand – didn't sound English.' Edward thought uncomfortably of the urgency with which he'd given him the message. He felt behind him in his jacket pocket to show Fen the scrap of paper, but as his fingers touched it he remembered his promise. He pushed it down again. 'I wish I knew who his son was.'

'Ask around. Someone in Uffenham may have

come across him – sounds as if he'd stand out. Try Miss Newnes. She's probably lived here forever.'

'Who?'

'Astrid Newnes. Lives in Neptune Alley with her two sisters. They've made the main figure for the Carnival float and some costumes, too. I'm no good at sewing, bores me stiff. Beats me why I'm always asked to organize a float each year.'

'You're good at it, that's why,' said Edward affectionately. He also knew how much Fen enjoyed grumbling about it afterwards.

She gave a snort, and her turban swayed.

'What are you doing for the float?' he asked nervously. He and Matt were usually roped in as extras. Last time the theme had been Julius Caesar arriving on the shores of Britain. Edward had been a Roman soldier in a toga as short as a hand towel, and his Daffy Duck boxers had showed.

'The Kingdom of the Sea God. There are boxes of the stuff sitting in one of the communal garages in Marine Street if you want to go and have a look.'

'I think I'll go and unpack just now, thanks,' he said hastily.

But Fen wasn't going to let him off so easily. 'I had a note from Astrid Newnes this morning. She and her sisters want to get the costumes out of their guest room. They do Bed and Breakfast in the summer, you see.' She looked at Edward with beady, expectant eyes. 'You're good with old ladies. A couple of trips to the Marine Street garage and you'll have cleared their room for them. And you can collect the figure of the sea god at the same time. I'm really pushed at the moment.' She tapped the flower painting. 'Three more of these to be done for the Captain's Cabin by the end of next week!'

'OK,' he said, resigned. 'I'll do it. So long as I don't have to talk to them!'

Fen flashed her tombstone teeth at him triumphantly. 'I said you'd go tomorrow morning. You'll charm them, I'm sure. Oh, it's good to have you and Matt here. I thought you mightn't come this year, that it would be just Hodder and me rattling around for the summer.'

Edward shifted his feet. A shadow passed over the kitchen. Fen opened her mouth as if she wanted to say more, looked at him, and shut it again. He thought he should respond with some polite comment, like 'It's great to be back', but it wasn't true, and they both knew why. In the end he gave her a clumsy nod, seized his jacket and went out of the kitchen without saying anything.

He hung the jacket on a peg in the tiny, dark hall. The message was safe in the pocket; he'd leave it there for the time being. Then, full of dread, he went up the narrow staircase, expecting to find Matt lying in a morose heap on his bed. Instead, he was whirling clothes with great enthusiasm from his bag into the open drawers of the chest.

'Hi,' said Edward uncertainly, shutting the door of the back bedroom behind him.

Matt's eyes were sparkling. 'You've been ages. You missed her.'

'Who?'

'Vali. I met her in the High Street. She's back, too. Over from Norway for the summer.'

Edward's heart sank. He didn't like Vali, and last summer and the summer before that, Matt hadn't either. 'Why's *she* back?'

'She's looking after those Price twins again. It's to improve her English. She says she's forgotten it all in the last year but it still sounds pretty smooth to me. She's in with a cool new crowd here, apparently.' Matt threw himself back on his bed so that his feet banged against the footboard, and propped himself against the pillows, smiling into space.

Edward went over to the chest and emptied his pockets of the stones. They rattled out on to the wood, slate blue, grey, two pinkish ones, the flat green stone and some oddly shaped ones he'd liked. They left wet marks where they lay on the top of the chest, and sand spilled from his empty pockets, gritting under his feet.

'Hey! You've brought in half the beach!' But Matt's protest was only half-hearted. He was still in his good mood. He watched Edward lazily as he examined the stones. 'I thought I heard that old man say something to you?'

'He gave me a message. I've got to give it to his son.'

'Let's have a look.'

'It's in my jacket pocket downstairs. Anyway,' Edward added hastily, 'you won't be able to read it. I don't think it's written in English.'

'Who's his son?'

'He didn't tell me. He disappeared, just like that. I don't know his son's name or anything about him!'

'Crazy.'

'He said his son would know *me*. What did he mean, d'you think?'

Matt stretched his arms above his head. 'One lunatic recognizing another, probably.'

'Get off!' They grinned at each other.

'From the back . . .' Edward said hesitantly, '. . . that jacket . . . He did look like Dad, didn't he?'

'I suppose.'

'I keep thinking. We don't know anything for sure, do we? I mean, they never found Dad's body, did they?'

The familiar darkness clouded Matt's face. 'Do you think I haven't thought about that all this year? But he didn't have a chance. Sailing single-handed out at sea, and a bloody great storm round his ears!'

'But they found the boat!'

Matt drew his long legs up with a violent movement and hunched himself over them. 'Look, do you want me to go through all the things that can go wrong in bad weather in a small boat? I've gone over and over all the reasons Dad might have drowned. I know them by heart. Well, do you?'

'No.'

'Then shut up about it!'

Edward kept quiet. He unzipped his bag, pulled out T-shirts, sweaters and jeans, and went over to the chest of drawers. The colours of the stones had become matt and faded as they dried.

'Get those stones off the top!'

Silently, Edward took them off the chest and laid them along the windowsill, in a neat row, like a line of traffic.

'Not there, you wally! We've got to pull the blinds down!'

'But there's nowhere else.'

Edward stood his ground, unexpectedly stubborn. They were good stones. He'd chosen carefully. He might even paint them in secret some time. *Still Life with Stones* by Edward Hodder.

Matt leapt off the bed and went to the windowsill. One by one he picked up the stones and dropped them into the wastepaper basket, holding them deliberately high in the air and letting them fall with a clunk on to each other. They were heavy. One or two broke cleanly in half as they landed. As he dropped them, he watched Edward's face. His eyes glinted and he smiled a mean little smile, waiting to see how Edward would retaliate, waiting for – wanting – a fight.

Then he cursed as he dropped the last one and cradled his hand to his chest. 'You've got a knife amongst that lot!'

He held out his hand and they looked at it in amazement. Blood was seeping slowly from a long, shallow cut across the palm. It had left a small but bright red stain on his white T-shirt.

Edward was speechless. So was Matt. Then Edward bent down and stared at the stones in the wastepaper basket. The flat green stone lay on top of the others, unbroken. It gleamed in the late afternoon light.

'It was that stone, the one on top!' Matt nursed his hand. 'The end's as sharp as a blade!'

'I didn't notice when I picked it up,' said Edward defensively. He turned out his pockets again, mystified. 'It hasn't even made a hole. Weird! Let's have a look at it.'

He bent forward to take the stone out of the basket.

'Leave it there!' said Matt. 'It's not a stone, it's a weapon! I'm going to find a plaster.' The bedroom door slammed behind him.

Edward shoved his clothes into the bottom two drawers of the chest, the drawers Matt hadn't taken. Then he leaned forward and gingerly took the stone out of the wastepaper basket between his finger and thumb. It was a glowing, transparent green now it was dry; it hadn't lost its colour like the others. He couldn't throw away something so beautiful. He'd have a proper look at it when he was on his own.

Quickly, before Matt came back into the bedroom, he wrapped the stone in a T-shirt and pushed the bundle away under his clothes in the bottom drawer of the chest.

For supper Fen had changed out of her smock and removed her turban, so that her hair, short, thick and dark, sprang up as if surprised at its freedom. She was wearing her celebration caftan. She always wore it the first night the boys were back at Uffenham. As she took saucepans off the stove, it billowed about her bony frame like a tent in a high wind.

'OK, guys, let's eat. God knows what time Hodder will be back.' She ladled out three generous portions of spaghetti and sat down. 'Pity your mum couldn't make it this summer.'

'She's in a new job,' said Edward. 'She said she couldn't take a holiday so soon.'

Matt sighed elaborately. 'She didn't *want* to come, Edward.'

'Perhaps she'll manage a weekend later on,' said Fen cheerfully. 'Incidentally, how did your exams go, Matt? I've been meaning to ask since you arrived. When do you get the results?'

Matt's usual guarded expression relaxed as he answered her. He was wearing a clean T-shirt instead of the blood-stained one, and there was a plaster on his hand.

'Three weeks or so.'

'Worried?'

Matt shrugged. 'Doesn't really matter.' He frowned down at his plate.

'They'll be 'A's, Matt, you know they will,' said Edward. 'You don't have to worry.'

'Then it will be A levels, university, a doctorate, I expect,' sighed Fen. 'What it is to have a brilliant almost-nephew!'

'Don't bank on it,' said Matt. 'Not on the university and doctorate bit. I don't think I'll go in for all that.'

Edward stopped eating. 'Aren't you going to be an archaeologist, then? You've always wanted to be an archaeologist, like Dad.'

'No, Edward. *Dad* wanted it,' said Matt quietly. His fingers clenched on his fork and he dug at his spaghetti. 'Everyone's always pushing me. Dad was the worst.'

'How can you say that?' cried Edward.

'No problem. Dad's not here any more, is he? Well and truly out of the way.'

Fen intervened calmly. 'Matt's got plenty of time to decide on his future. There's too much pressure these days. Anyone want more spaghetti? Matt, dish it out for me, will you?'

While Matt's back was turned she leaned across and put a warm, knobbly hand over Edward's agitated one, giving it a squeeze. Out loud she said, 'I can see I'm going to have to cook gargantuan meals to fill up those enormous stomachs of yours!'

'Lay off!' protested Matt. He grinned at her over his shoulder, his mood evaporated. 'Anyway, if you do that, you won't have time to paint!'

'And then you won't have money from the sales of your pictures to do the shopping,' pointed out Edward, cheered by the pressure of Fen's hand.

'And who said *I* was going to do the shopping?' demanded Fen. 'Now I've got two men here with man-sized muscles, I shall sit back!'

They were arguing amiably when Uncle Hodder arrived. There was no evening sun outside, but he was wearing dark glasses. He looked grey with fatigue, and when he took his glasses off his eyes were dull and heavy-lidded. He sat down at the kitchen table at the end he always sat at, the end that had been opposite Dad's place. He looked at Matt's fair hair and an expression of pain passed fleetingly over his face. Edward, watching both of them, thought he knew why. It was because Matt was so like Dad to look at: fair, blue-eyed, vibrating with restless energy. But Matt's mouth, with its bitter and scornful twist, wasn't like Dad's any more.

Fen gave him a plate of spaghetti. 'Good auction, Hodder? Anything interesting?'

'Not much. One or two early editions. No firsts. Still, I bought a few books. Come to the shop sometime, boys, come and have a look around.'

Fen's cockscomb of hair bristled. 'They don't want *books*, Hodder! They have quite enough of those at school! Take some time off with them, you deserve it. Go swimming with them, sailing—'

'Not sailing, if you don't mind,' said Matt tersely.

Fen bit her lip. 'I'm sorry. Well, you've got the car, Hodder. Take the boys on a day trip somewhere. There's Adventure World further up the coast, or that Saxon castle at Burgh if you want culture, or even Uffling Hoo on our own doorstep.'

Matt laughed, and the tension was broken. 'Hang on, Fen! We don't need amusing, do we, Ed? We're family, not guests, remember?'

Family, with one person missing.

Edward was conscious now of the solid emptiness Dad's chair held, the electric light brightness that showed the gap at the other end of the table. His food stuck in his mouth and it was hard to get through the rest of the supper.

Afterwards, they all watched television in the front room. Then Edward muttered something about going to bed early and left them sitting there.

'You'll get the breakfast bread for me, tomorrow morning, same as usual?' Fen called up the stairs after him. She was offering him comfort. Getting freshly baked bread from the baker's in the High Street was Edward's usual job during Uffenham holidays.

But this holiday wasn't the same as usual, and there was no comfort.

He was in his bed, listening to CDs, when Matt crashed in much later. Matt's hair was windswept, his cheeks flushed with cold air.

'Where've you been?' asked Edward sleepily, taking his headphones off.

Matt started to undress, pulling off his sweater. Edward thought he wasn't going to bother to answer, but when he emerged, he said shortly, 'I was on the beach. Thinking about things.'

'Oh,' said Edward, cautiously.

Matt's dark figure on the beach, staring at the dark sea. Had he been thinking about his future? About *not* being an archaeologist? Edward didn't want to talk about it now. He wanted his world secure about him for sleep. He turned his CD player off and eased himself further down under the warmth of the duvet.

Matt sat down on the other bed. He had pulled on his bedtime T-shirt and boxer shorts. They were too small, and his arms and legs poked out, looking endlessly long. His whole body was tense, quivering, but that was quite normal for Matt. The bedside light made one half of his face shadowy, so that Edward, under sleepy eyelids, could not read his expression.

'I was thinking about *him*.'

'Who?'

'Hodder.' Matt said it as though he despised the way their uncle had always preferred being called by his surname.

'What about him?' said Edward.

'I was thinking – he's our father-figure now, Uncle Hodder with his dusty books and papers, who knows more about life a couple of centuries ago than now!'

'It's his work,' mumbled Edward, yawning. 'He can't help it. It's what he's interested in.'

'He's a loser, and he knows it,' said Matt savagely. 'Some role model! I think Fen earns more than he does. At least she doesn't stay stuck in Uffenham all the time.'

'I like Uffenham,' murmured Edward, 'I'd like to be stuck here,' but Matt swept on.

'He's lost his grip, you can tell it, can't you? Do you know why?' Matt bent closer, so that his breath steamed on Edward's cheek. 'Shall I tell you what Fen told me once?'

Edward's eyes jerked open.

'What?'

'Hodder was jealous of Dad.'

'*What?*'

'She didn't exactly say that, of course. But she meant it. She was laughing, making it a joke. She said Hodder would like his name known too, get on the telly, have a series to himself, like Dad. It might bring the bookshop more customers.'

'So? What does that mean?'

'Dad was well-known, wasn't he? It wasn't just bringing archaeology to the masses on TV. I didn't realize how respected he was until I saw those obituaries. Hodder could never make it like that. The owner of a little antiquarian bookshop in Woodbridge famous? No way! That was when Hodder . . . when Hodder first started thinking he'd had enough.'

'Enough of what?'

'Enough of Dad.'

Edward pushed himself up on his elbows in bed. He wasn't sleepy any more. The room was cold, choked with sea air from the open window. He stared at the lit part of Matt's face and it told him nothing.

'What are you talking about?' His voice sounded thin.

'My theory. It's only a theory, but I like theories. It came to me on the beach, just like that. You see, it was Hodder's boat that Dad went sailing in. Hodder lent it to him. But he didn't go with Dad. And Dad . . . never came back.'

Although Matt spoke softly, the words thumped down. Edward stared at Matt, and Matt stared back at him. Then Matt slid his eyes away from Edward's. He fiddled with the plaster on his palm. The blood from the cut had soaked through, staining it brown.

Edward managed to speak. 'That's crazy! You can't . . . You surely don't believe that—'

Indignation burst through him. He felt his whole conception of things tremble like a blown bubble.

Then, at last, Matt lifted his gaze from his plastered hand. He turned towards Edward, and the light fell fully on his face. His expression was ashamed, almost alarmed. 'Sorry, Ed. I've been talking a load of rubbish. The beach was full of shadows—' His voice faltered. 'I didn't mean any of that. Forget I ever said anything.' He nursed his hand. 'God, this cut hurts like hell. Has done all evening.'

He got up abruptly and went out of the room. Edward waited, lying stiffly under his duvet. He heard the flush go in the bathroom, the sound of running water. But when Matt came back, he turned the light off without saying anything more, and climbed beneath his own duvet, pulling it up to his chin. In the summer half-darkness, Edward could see his head turned away on the pillow. He didn't dare say anything.

Uncle Hodder was no substitute for Dad, it was true. Dad had been outgoing, always talking, always the leader. Uncle Hodder had been a shadow in the sunlight round Dad. He'd always found it difficult to know what to say to his nephews, how to treat them. Edward recognized that shyness in himself, a gag that bound up the words. Now it was worse than ever, for them both.

But in spite of everything his uncle had still wanted them to come back this summer.

Tossing in bed, these thoughts going jerkily through his mind, a sudden picture came to Edward. His father's funeral. Uncle Hodder, grey and speechless, dark glasses covering his eyes. He hadn't wanted people to see him crying, that was why. And he still wore those dark glasses outside now, so that people shouldn't look too closely at his sadness.

He'd loved Dad, his younger brother, and Matt knew that; in his deepest heart he knew that just as clearly as Edward did. What had got into him tonight?

CHAPTER THREE

The Walker From the Beach

Early the next morning, Edward came out of the baker's with a large loaf of new bread in a paper bag. He wandered down a side street to the sea front. No one would be awake yet back at the cottage, and he liked this time of day best at Uffenham, when it was still empty of trippers and on the beach there were only fishermen pulling up their boats.

The sea front, which was grandly called the Parade, was lined with tall, narrow houses of red brick, the white paint peeling on their wooden balconies. They had been converted into holiday flats and were shut in winter, but they didn't look so very lived-in now, at the beginning of August. Clutching the bag of warm bread against his chest, he swung his legs over the low concrete wall that edged the far side of the Parade and jumped down on to the beach. He'd lob a few pebbles into the water before he went back to breakfast, see if he could still skim the waves with them.

The sea and the sky were the same pale, shining silver, and there was no horizon. It was like being inside a glass bowl, he thought, as he crunched down over the shingle to the water's edge.

Plop. He threw a pebble. *Plop*. Each stone was swallowed with a minute sucking noise, hardly clipping the delicate curl of the waves. They unrolled slowly across the shingle in one continuous line, like a spool of gauze. Watching the waves, Edward forgot Matt's dark whisperings of the night before; he felt as clean and empty as the morning.

He pushed his left hand down into his jacket pocket as he stood there, and the scrap of paper with its one-word message curled round his fingers, almost warm against his damp flesh. He pulled the paper out and examined it again. A pencil scrawl that could be any word at all, any word in any language. But a secret word so significant that other people wanted to know it. And he was entrusted to pass it on.

The harsh, desperate voice from yesterday cracked the quiet in his head and filled him with anxiety. He must be on the lookout for anyone who might be the old man's son.

It had become colder as he stood on the shingle, trying to puzzle out the word. When he looked up he could see the rim of the sea; the clouds were dark and separate and below them the sea had turned to pewter.

What was that on the horizon?

He strained his eyes. He was staring at the solid lump of a land mass where he knew none existed, not for miles and miles, anyway. Yet there on the horizon were the unmistakable shapes of mountains, of snow-capped peaks, glaciers ... He could see glittering towers and palaces of ice. On his lips was the powdery numbness of frost.

He rubbed a hand across his eyes and when he took it away the island was still there, as if it drifted on the surface of the sea. It must be cloud, a cloud shadowing the horizon, that was all.

But suddenly he was filled with hope. If Dad hadn't been drowned in the storm last summer, he might have been blown somewhere else in the boat. What if he had reached dry land safely and had disembarked on that strange shore, leaving the boat to drift back by itself? What if Dad all this time was safe somewhere else entirely, somewhere that no one knew about?

In your dreams.

He tucked the message carefully back into his pocket, turned his back on the cloud-island and headed back to Gull Cottage and breakfast.

* * *

Matt didn't emerge from the back bedroom for breakfast. Shortly afterwards Uncle Hodder left for Woodbridge, with dark glasses covering his eyes again though the sun had not emerged.

Fen turned brightly towards Edward. 'What are you up to today? The Walters are back at North Path Cottage. I could do you and Daniel a picnic.'

'It's OK, thanks.' *I must find the old man's son*, he thought. It felt reassuring to have a project, and not to mooch about, imagining Dad everywhere.

Fen wiped the work surface, then turned and looked at him for a long moment. 'You're too like your uncle, you know. Don't freeze other people out. You must see your old friends, Ed. You can't spend this summer alone.'

'I won't!'

'And you won't forget to go to the Newneses' this morning, will you?'

'No.'

'The key to the Marine Street garage is on the hall shelf.' Fen looked as if she wanted to say something else, but to Edward's relief there was a ring on the doorbell.

'I'll get it.'

He went through into the tiny hall and opened the front door. A girl he knew all too well, a girl a couple of years older than Matt, was standing on the doorstep, towering over him. She had silvery-blonde hair cut in a helmet shape round her head, and was wearing a white top over black jeans. One hand held a sports bag in shiny black parachute material, the other brandished a tennis racquet. She looked, to Edward, like a victorious goddess coming to claim her spoils.

'Hi, Vali,' he said nervously.

Vali's steel-grey eyes flickered over him. 'Where is Matt?'

'Still in bed,' said Edward, relieved. For a desperate moment he'd wondered if she'd come to practise her English on him.

'In bed?' She seemed nonplussed by this information. 'But we are to play tennis. I have the morning off.'

'Matt never gets up till about twelve,' he offered helpfully, and tried to close the door.

'Then you and I, little Edward, we shall play tennis together.'

'Me?' he said, aghast.

She eyed him sternly. 'Exercise is good for you, Edward.'

'Good idea, Vali,' shouted Fen from the kitchen. 'I was just saying to Edward I thought he should see some friends.'

'But I haven't got a tennis racquet here!'

'You can borrow mine,' said Fen cheerfully, appearing behind him. 'Haven't used it for about twenty-five years but it's as good as new. I'll get it for you.'

Fen's tennis racquet was screwed into a sort of wooden armour. Edward took it dumbly. A sinking feeling had taken him over. 'But I'm meant to be collecting that stuff for the Carnival float this morning!'

'You've plenty of time. It's only ten o'clock.'

Vali was already striding off down the High Street in the direction of the town steps, her black-jeaned legs flashing. Several male passers-by of varying ages looked after her admiringly. She glanced back at Edward and beckoned with an impatient swoop of the tennis racquet. There was nothing for it but to obey.

The message! He grabbed his jacket from the hall peg and flung it on, checking the paper was in the pocket. Outside there was the usual wind blowing, but today it brought gusts of hot air, too hot for wearing anything extra. Fen's antique tennis racquet was leaden in Edward's sweating grip as he toiled up the town steps after Vali. The public tennis courts were at the top, behind the library.

He wasn't looking where he was going, just frowning down at the steps under his feet and counting grimly to himself – 'twenty-seven, twenty-eight' – and that was how he almost collided with someone coming down.

He saw the shoes first. Heavy black shoes. City shoes.

Edward stopped, just avoiding the man. He saw the dark-grey city suit, but today the jacket was off and slung over one arm. It must be – it was – the walker from the beach yesterday. But there seemed to be no recognition in the narrow, intelligent eyes that glanced at him and then down at the High Street, as the man went on his way, nimbly running down the steps.

Then to Edward's consternation, he turned and began to spring back up towards him. 'Excuse me!'

At the man's call, Edward's heart began to beat stupidly, uncomfortably fast, and it wasn't from climbing. He remembered the raised arm, black against the sun. In his jacket pocket the message seemed to crackle incriminatingly. He stopped, rooted to the spot, trapped in the middle of the town steps.

The man climbed up closer to Edward. His face was handsome yet disturbing, as if the two halves of it did not quite match, were off-centre. He looked very hot, with a fiery tan that couldn't have come from sitting in an office; even his eyes, though blue, seemed to burn with heat. His hair was a dark, burnished auburn and bristled like the fur on an angry cat. But his voice, as he addressed Edward, was polite and full of charm.

'Excuse me, this is a long shot but I wonder if you

know some people called Newnes? Three elderly sisters? They live in Uffenham. I'm trying to find them.'

Edward's mouth opened in surprise. Before he could think, the words had come. 'My aunt knows them. They live in Neptune Alley.'

The man smiled. When he smiled, a great many lines creased the reddish-brown skin at the corners of his eyes as if he laughed a lot, but Edward had an odd feeling that what the man thought funny was not always so to other people.

'Thanks, that's very helpful. Uffenham's such a friendly place, isn't it? Everyone knows everyone.'

Then he turned with great agility on the narrow step and was off again down to the High Street, taking two steps at once with long, loping strides.

Edward stared after him uneasily. He didn't want to bump into him again at the Newnes sisters'. Strange that he should be looking for *them*, of all the people in Uffenham.

'Come, Edward!' Vali called, from the top of the steps.

After that it was difficult to concentrate on playing tennis. They stopped when Vali, still looking as cool as iced milk, began to complain of the heat. She had taken off her white top and was wearing what looked to Edward like a lacy breastplate underneath. He put down Fen's racquet and massaged his right wrist glumly, wondering if it would ever feel as if it belonged to the rest of his arm again.

'Let's get ice creams,' he suggested, hoping Vali wasn't on a diet like most girls he came across. 'I saw a van by the library.'

Vali wasn't on a diet. She decapitated her cone with one dismissive lick. 'The weather is not so hot in Norway.'

'It's not often like this in Uffenham! Is it never hot in Norway?'

She shook her head. Her helmet of fair hair quivered and settled once more into place around her smooth, stern cheeks. 'Not like this today. You should come to Norway in winter, Edward, then is the time. Ice and snow and mountains.'

'Ice and snow and mountains,' he echoed, his mouth full of frozen slush from his disintegrating ice lolly. *An island of ice*.

'If you sailed off in a boat from here and went in a direct line across the sea,' he said casually, 'you wouldn't reach Norway, would you? You couldn't even see it from here, even on a clear day?'

Vali laughed deeply. 'No, no, little Edward, Norway is much up.'

'Further north, you mean,' he said, with dignity.

Back at the cottage Matt was dressed and downstairs. He looked thunderous as they came in.

'You are the heavy sleeper, Matt,' said Vali. 'You

have lazy bones. Edward has been my partner instead.'

Matt was goggling at the lacy breastplate. 'I'm sorry, Vali. Let's go now.' He looked as if he couldn't wait to get Vali out of the cottage and to himself.

'More tennis? In this weather? Are you crazy? A swim, yes.' She tapped her sports bag. 'I have my towel and swimsuit.'

'Great idea,' said Edward, hanging his jacket up with relief. 'I feel just like a swim.'

Matt glared at him. 'Fen said there was some job you'd promised to do for her. Hadn't you better do it now . . .' He came close to Edward and hissed into his ear, '. . . Or *die*!'

A few moments later Edward was walking down Marine Street feeling aggrieved. He hadn't even had time to splash water over his hot face before Matt had pushed him out; worse, he'd left the message behind in his jacket without transferring it to his jeans. Now if he spotted anyone likely to be the old man's son, he wouldn't have it on him.

A cat glared at him from a windowsill, so he grimaced hideously back at it. There was no one to see him in the stuffy little street with its row of closed cottage doors and narrow front gardens crowded with wilting hollyhocks. Everyone sensible was on the beach. He kept catching bright glimpses of the sea down the alleyways he passed.

As he turned into Neptune Alley, Edward saw a figure down the far end.

The man had his back to him and was walking away with his loping strides, still carrying the suit jacket over one arm. He disappeared round the far corner without looking back. Edward stepped cautiously into the alley, but to his enormous relief the man did not reappear.

The cottage was easy to spot, through an archway in the otherwise blank concrete wall of the alley. No name, no number, but it had a sun-faded notice in its front window, BED AND BREAKFAST. He crossed the little cobbled yard to the front door. There was no bell, but a knocker that felt very cold against his sticky palm.

The door was opened by a tall, wiry old woman with a bush of wild grey hair and an angry manner.

'Yes?'

'Er – I'm Edward Hodder,' he said, taken aback. 'My aunt—'

'We know who you are. Hurry up. You haven't much time.'

'I'm sorry. Am I late, then? I didn't know—'

She brushed aside his apology and opened the door further. He followed her meekly into a dark, narrow hall that smelled of the sea. There was a door at the far end but it was shut, and a flight of stairs to his left, up which he was motioned with a brisk wave.

'The guest room's on the left. Everything's in bags in there.'

She did not come up with him.

The landing was bigger than he expected, with four doors off it. Tentatively, he turned the nearest handle. To his horror another old woman was there, sitting surrounded by cushions on the bed in the middle of the room. She was fully dressed, in a fluffy sort of cardigan and skirt, but the curtains were drawn and he thought he must have woken her up.

'I'm sorry,' he repeated, stammering, 'I didn't meant to disturb you, but my aunt—'

To his relief she did not look nearly as fierce as the first Miss Newnes. As his eyes grew accustomed to the dimness, he saw she had a round, comfortable face, so smooth and unwrinkled that for a moment he thought she wasn't old at all. Her short white hair was held to one side with a child's pink plastic slide and her cheeks were plump, powdery purses on either side of her smiling mouth.

'I'm Mae. My elder sister, Zelma, said you were coming. It's so kind of you to clear the guest room for us. We do Bed and Breakfast, you know.' She gave a wistful little sigh. 'We're always hoping for a visitor.'

There were several bulging bags by the bed. The dimness in the room seemed to give everything a quivering, translucent quality, so that for a moment Edward thought he could see through the plastic of the bags to things that glittered and glowed inside: robes and circlets and jewellery. They made a shining wall beneath Mae's plump little feet, which dangled over the side of the bed in black strap shoes.

'I'll take one lot and then come back for the rest, if that's OK,' he said.

She nodded and clasped her soft white hands together. 'That's right, dear. What a good boy you are.'

As he bent down beside her to pick up the first bag, she glanced at him coyly. 'We knew you were the right one. We brought you here, you know.'

Mad, thought Edward, *seriously loopy*, as he went down the stairs with his first load.

Outside in Marine Street it was hotter than ever. The wind pushed warm, sticky air at him and rolled small pebbles into the gutters.

He unlocked the garage door and heaved it up over his head on its hinges. Fen's other helpers had been busy. There were several boxes in there already, and bulky shapes that he thought must be scenery, covered by black plastic and cloth. He put the bags down, and out of curiosity pulled out one of the costumes: a tunic with wide sleeves. He was surprised to see how professional it looked. Mae might be nutty, but she and her sisters could certainly sew.

She wasn't in the bedroom when he went back for the remaining bags. He remembered he had to collect the float's centre figure as well, but it wouldn't be among the lace frills and satin cushions of the bedroom. He stowed the bags with the others in the garage and returned reluctantly to Neptune Alley.

At the end of the narrow hall a door was ajar, as if waiting for him. He went over the damp-stained carpet. 'Excuse me . . .'

Shyness dried up his voice. Alarmingly he saw not just one sister, little Mae, inside the room, but the two others as well. The old women were sitting silently and all three were gazing straight at him: the brisk angry first one; Mae; and the third sister, Zelma.

Zelma was so ancient her features seemed blurred. Under the colourless folds of her cardigan her body seemed to drift about in a large armchair: she looked as though she would float up to the ceiling if it weren't for the chair anchoring her to the floor.

'Come, Edward.' It was only a whisper from the old woman but he heard it clearly. He came awkwardly into the room, which was dark and damp, and filled with an even stronger smell of the sea than the rest of the house.

'You've been a time,' growled the first Miss Newnes.

'Hush, Astrid. The poor boy's exhausted,' said Mae. She herself looked as fresh and creamy as a meringue. She was plumped in the other armchair, eating a sugar biscuit with relish. She passed the plate to Edward. 'There's always time, plenty of time. Certainly time for you to have a biscuit, my dear.'

'No, thank you,' said Edward politely, stuck with the plate and wondering what to do with it. Every surface seemed filled with clutter. He was longing to have a drink back at Gull Cottage, and the sight of the biscuits, crumbly and sugar-speckled, made his mouth feel drier than ever. 'I just wanted to say—'

'Plenty of time for you, perhaps,' Astrid snapped at Mae, just as if he hadn't spoken. 'Mine's all used up. It's all right for those who live in the *present*.'

'Girls, girls,' said Zelma, in her soft, whispery voice. She turned to Edward and her filmy gaze passed round and over him. 'There's a drink for you on the table there, if you'd like it.'

'Orange squash!' said Mae. She cocked her head with its slide and looked at Edward sideways. 'Isn't that what boys like? I went to the supermarket specially. So many bottles and cans to choose from, and such lovely colours. Oh, I did enjoy myself!'

'It's fine. Thanks.' He took the glass from the little table and somehow managed to manoeuvre the plate into the space it had taken, between a half-finished jigsaw and a bundle of bright pink wool and knitting needles.

His swallows seemed very loud to his embarrassed ears. There was only the ticking of the clock in the room, and a curious distant, swishing sound, like waves. The three old women were watching him, so he fixed his eyes hastily on the mantelpiece, looking at it through the rim of his glass as he drank. It was crowded with interesting things, and the glass seemed to magnify them: the clock, which was decorated with a design of sea serpents; a tiny ship with wings inside a glass bottle; a spike of crystal, clear as an icicle. Best of all was a glass-eye paperweight that goggled realistically from the far end of the shelf.

Then Astrid spoke, making him jump. 'Have you finished?' She wasn't sitting like her sisters any longer, but prowling round the room in a restless way. Now she was at his elbow.

He wedged his empty glass between the jigsaw and the plate of biscuits. 'Yes, thank you.' Perhaps he shouldn't ask them about the old man on the beach, after all. 'I'm also meant to collect a figure – for the float?'

'Take your time,' said Zelma. 'Mae will show you it in a minute.' She looked past him with her unsettling, dreamy gaze. 'I think you have a question for us first.'

45

Edward was taken aback. 'Well, yes – yes, I have. Someone I met yesterday. My aunt thought you might know him. A man – foreign, I think. Very tall, with a patch over one eye and . . .' he was not sure how to put it politely in the present company, '. . . er . . . old. The problem is that I never got his name, and he gave me a message for his son.'

Something passed between the three women, not a look, more a feeling. The distant pulse of the sea seemed to grow faster as they looked back at him: three pairs of old eyes watching him, weighing him up.

'Yes, we know him,' said Zelma.

'Does he live in Uffenham?'

'Live here?' snorted Astrid. 'Spends his time travelling, that one.'

'What about his son?'

'He'll be coming,' said Zelma, with strange conviction.

'I wish I knew what he looked like.'

'He'll know you,' she said gently. 'Wasn't that what you were told?'

'Yes, but—' He pulled himself together. 'But I don't see how he can. He's never met me. Do you know his name?'

Zelma did her disconcerting trick of looking past his head before she spoke. 'He'll tell you when he finds you, I'm sure of that.'

Edward hesitated, wondering how much to say about yesterday. 'Someone came up to the old man after he'd talked to me, the same man who came to see you just now.'

Astrid looked crosser than ever. 'See us, indeed! He can't find his way in. He's hunted us for years and never found us yet!'

'And never will, either,' said Mae gaily.

'It's not for you to know that, Mae. It's out of your time.'

'Sorry, Zelma, dear.'

Zelma smiled faintly at Edward. 'Now, it's time you let Edward have his sea god.'

He struggled to remember his manners as he stood up. 'I hope you'll all be able to come to the Carnival.'

'We have our ways,' said Mae. She cocked her chin at Astrid. 'My time for a little treat, I think.'

'*You* went to the supermarket!'

Mae ignored her and held up a soft hand to Edward. She hardly needed his support, nipping from her chair with surprising agility and barging past Astrid to lead him to a long curtain, half-hidden in the shadows of the room. She whisked it aside and opened a door behind it.

He found himself outside in the sunlight, standing in a tiny, paved square, surrounded by high walls. In one corner a white hollyhock grew from a clump of weedy grass and next to it stood a tall, silvery-green figure, wearing a helmet and covered with an armour of fish scales made from foil.

Edward had to tilt his head back to look up at the empty eye-holes. 'It's amazing!'

Mae patted her hair modestly. 'We'll see how he does in time.'

'It's Neptune, isn't it?'

'We have a different name for him.' She pointed down a narrow side passage that opened out at the front of the cottage. 'You can take him out that way.'

In spite of its height, the figure was hollow and weighed nothing. Supporting it carefully, Edward turned to say goodbye.

The mid-morning light showed Mae stout and elderly and over-made up, but when she blinked up at him her eyes were surprisingly shrewd. 'Poor boy. I heard you lost your father.' She squeezed his hand. 'Good luck with the finding.'

Was she still talking about Dad? Or finding the old man's son?

CHAPTER FOUR

Struggling With the Sea

Back at Gull Cottage, Matt was still out and Edward could hear a scuffling sound like a large, busy animal, coming from upstairs. Fen must be in the boxroom, sorting out her drawings.

Silently, he darted up the stairs, past the boxroom door and into the back bedroom. He pulled open the bottom drawer of the chest and unwrapped the T-shirt that held the stone. Somehow the cotton had already been torn by the stone's sharp point. Mum wouldn't be pleased when he got home. But the stone was amazing: like a shining green icicle; and there were lines through it that he hadn't noticed before, branching out from the centre the way the veins did on a leaf. When he held the stone up to the light, they flickered as if they pulsed with secret life.

He wrapped the stone up carefully again and hid it

away. It was special, and he was going to keep it whatever Matt said.

When he came out of the bedroom, Fen was on her way downstairs, a sketchbook in one hand. 'You came in quietly. I thought the Newnes sisters must have eaten you for their elevenses! How did you get on?'

He followed her into the kitchen. 'They're weird. Like three old witches.'

Fen put her sketchbook down on the table. 'The one I met was certainly formidable. She came up to me in the street one day and said she'd heard I needed help with our float.'

'Astrid? She's the youngest.'

'Good Lord! However old are the others?'

'Did you . . . did you say anything to her about Dad?'

'No, of course I didn't. Why?'

'They seemed to know, that's all.'

'People gossip, you know, Ed. Uffenham's a small place.'

He nodded, frowning, then helped himself to a biscuit from the tin. 'What I don't understand is how they can sew. I mean, they can't *see* all that well, and the oldest, Zelma, she's almost blind, I think. But the costumes are brilliant. I looked. And you should see the sea god!'

'I'll go and inspect them when I've got a moment. I must ring and thank them.'

'They won't be on the telephone, I bet. They haven't even got a telly!' Edward could see Fen was about to say something scathing about not everyone thinking television entirely necessary to their lives, so he took another biscuit to distract her. She rose to the bait at once.

'Hey, stop that! You'll ruin your lunch.'

He looked at the kitchen table, covered with her work. 'Is lunch ready then?' he asked innocently. 'I didn't realize.'

'It will be when you've helped me get it.'

He was obediently washing some lettuce when Fen said, 'Did you find out anything about your one-eyed stranger?'

He shook his head.

'Oh dear, I thought they'd be just the sort of people who'd know everyone in Uffenham. So it was a wasted morning.'

'Doesn't matter.'

Fen regarded him steadily for a moment, her brown eyes as sharp and round as a bird's. He knew that look. 'Tell you what,' she said brightly, 'come and do some sketching with me tomorrow on the marshes. I missed our sessions last summer. Ask Daniel to come along too if you want. We'll go early, maybe take breakfast. It'll be just like it used to be, won't it?'

* * *

'Vali's working this afternoon,' said Matt at lunch-time. He had come back from the beach in a foul mood.

'We could go swimming,' said Edward. 'I left my best penknife in the bathing hut last year. I'd like to find it again.'

'I don't mind what you both do,' said Fen, 'so long as you leave me in peace. This afternoon's the deadline for this painting.'

It was oppressively hot outside, even though they were only wearing T-shirts and swimming trunks. Edward clapped his hand to his side. 'I haven't brought the message!'

'You're not still banging on about that, are you?'

'But I might meet the old man's son!'

Matt was obviously not in the mood to turn back. Anyway, Edward had no pocket to keep the message safe. He worried over it while Matt bought them ice creams, then followed him out of the High Street on to the Parade. The sky over the sea had turned a sullen yellow.

'Have you met Vali's new friends yet?' said Edward.

'She can keep them.' Matt kicked at a stone. 'They turned up on the beach. One of them fancies her, I can tell. Fancies himself, too. Wolf, he calls himself. His sister talked girl stuff with Vali all morning.'

Edward kept quiet and licked his second ice cream of the day. He checked the horizon. No sign of the cloud-island now. At his side Matt sloped moodily along looking as if Edward was nothing to do with him at all, one clenched fist gripping his bundled towel. A warm, sticky wind tugged at their hair; below them, the waves were plumed with white.

'There's the hut,' said Matt sounding almost cheerful suddenly. 'See? Still standing. Good old Number Fourteen. Race you there.'

He had already started off across the shingle and when Edward caught up with him, he was unlocking the door. He pulled it open with difficulty. It was stuck with sand. The air inside smelt of brine, old rubber and wood; against their faces it was almost solid with heat.

They let the wind blow in. Edward caught sight of Dad's old canvas bathing shoes in a corner, and his heart did a strange queasy jump. He looked away quickly, at Fen's vivid towelling robe on its peg, his and Matt's old water wings, the collapsed lilo under the window: all familiar, yet new, after a year of not seeing them. Someone had taken Dad's towel away but the penknife was still on the salt-stained windowsill.

Matt was tramping round and round on the small rectangle of wooden boards, looking carefully at everything, then again.

'Funny that it's still the same, isn't it? It should be different. Like everything else.' He stopped pacing and looked at Edward. 'I don't feel I know anything any more. It's as if everything I've ever done, everything I ever wanted was because of Dad, and now he's gone . . .' his face twisted, '. . . I'm nothing.'

Edward stared at him, aghast. 'You're not nothing. You're clever. What about the scholarship? You got that.'

'Dad pushed me into doing that, Edward. Didn't you realize? That's what I mean. I wouldn't have had the courage without him. And now he's not here, there's nobody to make me do anything. I should be pleased, shouldn't I?' Matt's eyes were as bruised and dark as Uncle Hodder's. 'But I don't know what to do any more.'

Edward was speechless. Matt's face changed. He gave his new, twisted smile. 'You always worshipped Dad, didn't you, Edward? You didn't realize how he took people over, Mum, me. Nor did I, till I was older than you, not till I took that scholarship.'

What he was saying in that place was blasphemous. Edward did not want to look at Dad's shoes, empty but pointing straight at him.

'For you he couldn't do a thing wrong,' said Matt. 'He was a god, wasn't he? A great big shining god!'

Edward put his hands over his ears. To his own amazement he heard himself scream: suddenly, shockingly. 'Shut up! Shut up! *Shut up!*'

When he opened his eyes, Matt had gone. He sat down, crouching into himself. He sat there for an age, while ice gathered round his heart, sealing off the feelings. He felt it spread to all his limbs so that they became cold, heavy, free of pain. Nothing could touch him now. He was an ice boy.

It was a long time before he became conscious of the wind, lifting his hair as it blew in through the open door. He stood up and went out of the hut, shutting the door carefully behind him. The waves were pounding up over the shingle, pushing almost to his feet before they spilled over into a dying froth of bubbles.

Edward walked down the beach into the sea.

He held on to a breakwater. It was wet under his hand. He took one step forward, holding on, then another. The water foamed round his ankles. There was spray on his face. He moved on, slowly, deliberately; all the time creeping his hand further along the breakwater. Beneath him, the sliding shingle sucked at his trainers.

He couldn't move. His hand was clenched so tightly on the wood of the breakwater he couldn't move back. The only way to go seemed forward, deeper. There was water churning all around him, and far below the surface his feet were drowned by stones.

This is what Dad felt, he thought, and he felt the terrible heart of the sea beat through him. *All I have to do is to let go.*

In that instant, his body seemed to jerk back by itself. He staggered, breaking his grip on the wood, almost falling; then he seized the breakwater again and dragged himself up. Pulling himself along hand over hand, he waded back with all his strength against the weight of water.

He had reached the dry shingle. He was safe!

He slumped down, rubbing his eyes clear of salt water with shaking hands. His swimming trunks and T-shirt were soaking, his thighs gooseflesh, quivering with cold. *I must get dry*, he thought, but he had to think it several times before he could struggle to his feet.

He took a step, oozing water from his trainers, then he saw.

Someone was in the sea, not far out: a figure tossed up to the peak of a wave, then hidden in the trough. Again, a flash of white limbs in the sour yellow-green water, an arm raised. Was it a signal for help?

Edward stood where he was, paralysed. He couldn't take his eyes from the struggling figure. A wave engulfed it, then it reappeared, closer in. It was swimming strongly, making headway to the shore. Was it going to make it? Another peak, the wave toppled, and then in a shower of spray and little stones, the swimmer was swept on to the beach, almost at Edward's feet.

Yes!

Edward squelched forward, jubilant with the swimmer's victory, as if he'd helped in it himself. He shouted to be heard above the wind. 'Are you OK?'

The swimmer lay there, gasping, face down on the stones. It was a man, in swimming trunks. His bare back heaved, gleaming with drops of water. The hope died in Edward as quickly as it had flickered. It wasn't Dad, of course; it wasn't Dad's stocky, tanned body. This man was big and his long limbs were pale, as if they'd been sculpted from marble.

He looked around, but there was nothing that might belong to a swimmer anywhere on the shingle – no pile of clothes, no towel – and all the bathing huts looked closed up. He shivered in sympathy, remembering the cold, cold sea.

'Are you OK?' he repeated, after what seemed a long time filled with the man's gasps and grunts. He wondered desperately if he should do anything and if so, what. He'd chickened out of the life-saving classes at the local swimming pool: kiss of life, all that embarrassing stuff.

He squelched closer and bent down gingerly over the prone figure. The gasping seemed to have stopped. Edward was appalled. Was he going to die on him now? Miles and miles of empty shingle and just him and a dead body in the middle of it all. *God, please not!*

The man rolled over and opened his eyes.

CHAPTER FIVE

The Wrong One

His face was young and smooth, apart from golden stubble round the chin. Fair hair was plastered over his forehead, like seaweed. He pushed it from his face with a large hand and grunted something. His whole muscular frame was shivering violently.

Large drops of rain had begun to fall from a leaden sky. Far off over the sea there was a flash of sheet lightning.

'Come on!' said Edward, taking a limp arm and tugging. The young man mumbled something and staggered to his feet. Together they stumbled up the beach, Edward steering him towards the bathing hut.

He pulled the door shut behind them and they collapsed on the floor. Warm air closed round them like a blanket. After a few minutes he draped a towel gingerly over the young man, who was slumped motionless with his eyes shut. The towel only just covered his back and looked rather small and mean, so he put another one over his legs and another on his feet. That used up all the towels; there was only Fen's beach robe left. He enveloped himself in it and sat down to get warm.

The rain clanged on the tin roof. It didn't seem to disturb the swimmer. Had he died after all?

Edward had begun to panic by the time the rain softened to a patter above them. The storm was moving away. Then suddenly the young man opened his eyes.

For a second they stared at each other. Then the swimmer ran his tongue over his lips. He tried to croak something.

'I've got nothing to drink here,' said Edward apologetically.

The man shook his head. He was grey-faced with exhaustion but his eyes, though bloodshot from swimming, were mesmeric; the light blue of northern skies. Edward was struck by the brilliance of his gaze before he covered his face with his hands. He sat there, and Edward sat too, waiting. Strangely, he didn't feel nervous. A gentleness seemed to emanate from the swimmer. Peace stole over Edward almost without his knowing it.

Then the young man shot out one of his huge hands and gripped his arm. Edward gasped and shrank back, his heart beating wildly.

As suddenly, the man released his arm and moved away against the wall. Edward crouched, staring, not daring to move.

Grunting with the effort, the young man pulled himself up against the windowsill, scattering towels like confetti. He gestured at Edward, pointing at the salt-caked window. What was it? What did he want him to see? Was he mad?

The man licked a finger and began to move it slowly, laboriously, over the clouded glass. He beckoned to Edward with a swift, imperious movement of his hand. There was something in that gesture that reminded him suddenly and startlingly of the old man on the beach yesterday: the same impatience, the same urgency.

Edward held his breath. He moved cautiously to the window, ready to fly should the other make any move. But the young man stood back to let Edward see, and where the salt had been rubbed away on the glass, the light shone through smeared writing. He could only make out three letters.

BUR

The young man pointed at himself, at his muscular chest, then Edward was offered a huge hand. He shook the hand uncertainly; it made his palm tingle. Bur? Was that the swimmer's name, or just part of it? But with a groan, as if he had achieved all he could for the moment, the young

61

man slid down the wall and on to the towels.

Edward crouched beside him. 'My name's—'

The brilliant eyes fixed on him. 'I know who you are,' whispered the swimmer painfully, and he shut his eyes.

So the old man's son had found him. He knew who he was! Edward didn't understand how it was possible. All he knew was that he'd failed his own task: he'd left the vital message behind.

Edward knelt down by the young man under the window, in the greenish light reflected from the sea, and tugged some of the towels out from under him to cover him up again. He was sure he should be kept warm.

Sadness filled him suddenly. 'You came from the sea,' he whispered, 'but you're the wrong one. You should have been my father!'

And what was he to do with him now: a mysterious swimmer who'd conquered the storm and was almost dead with exhaustion? He couldn't stay here, in the bathing hut. He must have left some clothes somewhere. He must *live* somewhere. Should he bring him water, fetch a doctor? Perhaps he should tell Fen. She'd know what to do, she always did.

Edward gave the sleeping figure a trial poke. He – Bur? – didn't move. He felt quite warm through the towels, whereas Edward was beginning to feel chilly.

His swimming trunks were still damp and stuck clammily to his legs, and his trainers were like wet sponges.

The rain had stopped, and the only sound was the young man's breathing, almost in time with the rhythm of the surf on the shingle outside. Suddenly he shifted restlessly in his sleep, flinging one arm out and groaning. His lips moved. Rusty, strangulated words came out, but words that Edward could understand.

'In the great grey hall hang pillars of ice, and the bud grows dead on the world ash tree.'

Then a cry of anguish was torn from him, a desolate wail that eddied round and round the hut and chilled Edward's blood.

He flung off Fen's towelling robe, grabbed his penknife from the sill and made for the door. It opened with difficulty over the sandy step. He didn't look back to see if the man had woken himself with his cry. He shoved the door shut with his foot, and fled.

He was still running towards the Parade, not so fast now and thinking he'd been stupid to be scared of someone else's nightmare, when he almost crashed into a girl who must have been standing watching him for some time.

'Hi!' said the girl, and her freckled face split into a shy smile of pleasure. 'I thought it was you, but my glasses are all covered in salt.'

'Hi,' panted Edward. He couldn't face making polite conversation after what had just happened, especially not with Lyddie, Daniel Walters's younger sister. She'd hung around him on previous holidays like an eager puppy, anxious to please, always there when he and Daniel wanted to do things on their own. He couldn't even be flattered by her attention. She was over a year younger than him, chubby and a nuisance.

But he had a stitch. He bent over sideways, breathing hard.

'You're out of breath. Were you jogging?' said Lyddie, in concern.

'No!' She'd lost some weight, or maybe she was just taller, but her Save the Uffenham Lifeboat T-shirt was sad.

'Where are you going, then?' Behind the glasses her eyes pleaded for friendship.

'Back into Uffenham.'

'So am I.'

'Sorry, but I've got to run.'

'Wait, please wait, Ed.'

Something in her voice made him stop. She took her glasses off and began twisting them in her hands. 'We read in the newspapers – about the inquest and everything. I meant to write – so did Daniel – but we didn't know what to say.'

He couldn't bear the pity in her eyes. 'It's not true!'

'What?'

'It's not true! They didn't prove Dad was dead, they didn't prove anything! He's still alive somewhere, he's just . . . *lost*, that's all.'

He whirled round and began to run again, leaving her standing on the wet path staring after him.

'Where's Fen?' he asked Matt, in dismay.

The bedroom was pungent with the smell of Sirocco deodorant spray and Matt, in a clean sweatshirt, was making faces at himself in the mirror. Edward recognized the procedure. He must have found a new spot.

'She's gone up to the Captain's Cabin with her stuff.'

'When's she coming back?'

'Haven't a clue.'

Edward began to change out of his damp clothes, feeling weighed down with responsibility. For a moment he considered telling Matt about the swimmer, but Matt, still busy at the mirror, clearly had other things on his mind just now.

'You're not going out stinking like that, are you?' said Edward, better for being warm and dry at last.

Matt ignored the question. He checked the gelled points of his hair. 'Vali's texted me. I'm going to meet her from work. What happened to you? Thought you'd be back ages ago.'

'I got caught in the storm.'

'I thought you might have stayed out because you were upset,' said Matt awkwardly. 'You know – about what I said earlier.'

Edward shook his head.

'Look, we'll probably check out the Cross Keys later,' said Matt. 'Sit on the beach wall and have a drink. Come along if you want, Ed. I'll buy you a Coke.'

It was a grand gesture of apology. Having got it off his chest, Matt leapt towards the door. Then he paused, looking slightly sheepish. 'There's nothing you'd notice about my face this evening, is there?'

'I don't suppose Vali *darling* will think it much weirder than usual,' said Edward, following him out. They thundered down the stairs together. Matt put his jacket on in the little hall and rechecked his hair.

'Smooth!' said Edward. He looked at the row of pegs. 'Hey, where's my jacket?'

'Fen borrowed it to go up to the Captain's Cabin.'

'*What?*'

'She was going to cycle there, and it was drizzling. She wasn't going to wear it, of course, just wanted something waterproof to cover her precious paintings in the basket.' He smirked at Edward's appalled face, blew him a kiss and vanished round the front door.

Going to the Captain's Cabin would take too long,

decided Edward. He'd have to come back for the message when he'd sorted everything else.

He made a Thermos of strong, sweet tea in the kitchen and put it into a plastic bag, with a bread roll and an apple. Fen must have finished the biscuits at the same time as her painting, because the tin was empty. He grabbed another bread roll for himself. Then he was out of the cottage and along the High Street, cutting through one of the alleyways to the Parade. He followed it along, chewing the roll, his eyes automatically checking the horizon.

The air was cool after the storm. Puddles gleamed underfoot; a pallid sun glimmered over the sea. The sky was washed clean of cloud so that however hard he tried he couldn't conjure up the island again. But in his imagination the land of ice and snow was sharp and glittering, and standing alone on its shore was a tiny matchstick figure, black against all the whiteness.

Dad. Waiting for rescue. *Lost*.

Edward had almost reached the path and the scatter of fishermen's huts and was walking quickly, trying to avoid the strolling holidaymakers, when he sensed someone keeping pace at his side. He looked round and his heart gave a leap of shock.

It was the man in the suit, only he wasn't wearing the suit any longer but jeans and a sweater. He should have looked the same as the other tourists, but he didn't. The rain had washed the colour from everything around: the sea, the houses with their white, peeling paint, the people in pale mackintoshes pacing the Parade; against them he blazed with vitality, his hair and face glowing bronze.

'It's my young friend from this morning, isn't it?' He smiled the charming smile Edward remembered and his eyes twinkled, so that the lines at the corners creased his sunburnt cheeks. 'The one who directed me to the Miss Newneses'? I thought I recognized you.' He stopped, so that Edward had to stop too, and held out his hand. 'My name's Locke.'

Edward stuffed the roll into his pocket hastily. 'Mine's Edward Hodder.' Mr Locke's hand was hard and almost burningly hot. Vivid as a snapshot Edward saw him threatening Bur's father yesterday, his arm black against the sun.

'Know the Newnes sisters well, do you?'

'Not very, no,' said Edward cautiously.

'They're old acquaintances of mine. I thought I'd look them up while I was here. I must have missed their cottage, though. What number did you say it was?'

'I don't think it's got a number.' Edward went on talking quickly, to distract him. 'Are you staying here long?'

'Possibly. My three children are holidaying here and we've some things to do together.' He glanced at Edward. 'They're older than you, I think – teenagers.'

He leaned down and sunlight flickered over his auburn hair. 'Actually, I'm also watching out for a young relative of mine. He should be arriving any moment. I thought it would be nice to have a family get-together. The four of us – and him. That's why I wanted to find the Newnes sisters, to see if they'd heard any news. They know his father, you see.'

Edward stayed silent. He clutched the plastic bag with the Thermos of medicinal tea and kept his eyes lowered. Then in a casual way Mr Locke put a hand on his shoulder. Edward could feel it grip and burn through his sweatshirt; he was too nervous to move.

'If you come across him, let me know. I'll be waiting for you. Remember that.' He released Edward and laughed. The intelligent, pale blue eyes crinkled attractively at the corners. 'But I'll find him anyway, sniff him out.' He laughed. 'Yes, sniff him out!'

In a minute his lithe figure, walking swiftly, had left the Parade and was out of sight up an alley.

CHAPTER SIX

Hunted

The door of the bathing hut was still safely wedged shut. As Edward pulled it open, the low sun shone in, lighting the sleeping figure inside with gold. He tugged it shut behind him and the hut was plunged into half-darkness.

Edward tried the name timidly. 'Bur?' Eventually the brilliant blue eyes opened, as if it had travelled a long way before it was recognized. 'Someone's looking for you! You must wake up!'

The young man tried to croak something. Hastily, Edward fumbled in his bag and brought out the Thermos. Bur's hand dwarfed the little plastic cup filled with tea. He shook his head at the roll and the apple, and put his salt-caked lips to the cup. Shining drops ran down his chin into the golden stubble and dripped on to the floor, making dark stains on the wood.

'Thank you.' There was a dignity about him as he handed the cup back. Unlike his father he had no accent, but a strange, slow way of speaking, as if he were still asleep.

'This person . . .' said Edward urgently, '. . . his name's Locke. He says he's a relative.' He hesitated, and added, 'But he didn't seem very friendly towards your father yesterday.'

The eyes came awake at once and blazed at him. 'Locke? Did you tell him where I was?'

'No, I didn't. I thought – you might not want me to.'

Bur's eyes softened and he nodded, pulling his swollen lips into a smile that was more of a grimace.

'But who is he, this Mr Locke?'

There was a strange expression on the young man's face. 'He was once like a brother to my father,' he said hoarsely. 'Now his ways are evil.'

Edward stared at him in amazement, but Bur seemed serious. Misgivings filled him. 'I think I know why he's searching for you like this. You see, your father wrote a message for you yesterday and gave it to me. He said other people would like to know it but it was secret, just for you.'

Bur passed a hand over his eyes. 'I know the word,' he said in a puzzled way, 'but I never can remember it.'

'The worst thing is I haven't got it with me at the

moment. But I'm sure Locke wants it.'

'He will hunt me to the end anyway,' said Bur wearily.

It was a strange thing to say. This was more than some family quarrel, surely? But before Edward could ask anything, Bur put a finger to his lips.

They both sat there motionless in the warm, salty twilight of the hut. Edward tried not to breathe so he could hear better, but the only sound he could make out was the hushing of waves on the shingle. Then at last there was another sound, distant at first, then closer: the crunch of footsteps. Occasionally the steps paused; but then, relentlessly, they would start again, moving closer all the time.

Someone was walking along the line of beach huts. Someone was looking for them.

Frightened, Edward stared at Bur. He was gazing at the door, his expression grim and concentrated. The footsteps crunched closer, paused somewhere outside. Little stones rattled into silence.

Edward's heart hammered against his ribs. *A raised arm, black against the sun*. The steps trod slowly and deliberately all round the hut and stopped at the door.

The steps moved on.

Bur didn't move for a long time, not until the footsteps had died into the distance, then at last he relaxed back against the wall.

'Was that Locke?' whispered Edward, his heart still thumping.

Bur nodded. 'He'll trap me if I stay in here.' But he looked at the end of his strength. Even as Edward stared at him in alarm, he let his head drop down on to his chest as if to venture from the bathing hut was too great an effort.

Locke might come back any moment. He had to get Bur out, find somewhere safe for him to rest. Gull Cottage? But it didn't seem right to involve Fen and Uncle Hodder in someone else's feud – or worse.

We're always hoping for a visitor.

It was as if the sea outside had whispered the words into Edward's head. He leapt to his feet and the thud made Bur open his eyes again. 'I'll take you to the Newnes sisters! Your father knows them, and they don't like Locke either. You'll be safe there.'

Bur looked up at him, frowning slightly. 'I should look for my boat,' he muttered.

Edward didn't know what he was talking about. 'We must hurry!' he said.

Frustratingly slowly, Bur pulled himself up by the windowsill again. There seemed to be a lot of him in the little bathing hut, and what there was looked very naked, apart from his swimming trunks which hung in flimsy and chilly-looking folds around his legs.

'You can't go like that,' said Edward, 'not in Uffenham!' He looked round and thrust Fen's towelling robe at him. 'Here!'

Bur took it, looking bemused. The bright, swirling pinks and blues were strangely crude in his large hands. He looked helplessly at Edward.

Edward sighed. 'Like this.' He'd never had to dress an adult before. The belt only just went round Bur's generous waist, and he tied a granny knot with the ends.

Bur looked so comical, with his arms and legs sticking out like tree-trunks, that he had to smile in spite of his anxiety. Then he saw how cut and bruised his feet were from the shingle. Dad's old shoes lay in the corner. He reminded himself they were only bits of canvas and rubber, nothing more. He made Bur sit down again and he knelt down himself, fitting the shoes on his bare feet, quickly lacing them up for him. For a moment he felt Bur's hand rest lightly on his head.

The shoes were a perfect fit.

Bur's face was greenish-white, the hair on his forehead damp, by the time he had dragged him out of the Parade, down Fishers Alley and into Marine Street. Leaving the stuffy dimness of the hut hadn't revived him at all. The cool air and pale, bright sunlight seemed to make him sleepier than ever.

He almost flattened Edward as he leaned on him, yawning and groaning. Edward was sure they must stick out amongst the ordinary tourists, a boy supporting a hefty young man in a lady's beach robe. But there was no sign of Locke, and no one else showed any curiosity.

There at last was the opening to Neptune Alley, and no one was around to notice him pull Bur towards it. Through the archway the cottage looked shabbier and more insignificant than ever, but the notice was like a welcoming beacon in the window: BED AND BREAKFAST.

With relief Edward heaped Bur against the brickwork of the cottage, and went to ring the doorbell. The door opened at last and the two younger Miss Newneses stood staring at him, the sunlight cruel on their faces.

'We may be old, but we're not deaf!' snapped Astrid, angry as ever.

'Hush, sister,' said Mae, still puffing from her walk down the hall. 'See. He's brought him.'

Astrid's fierce eyes left Edward. For a second the sisters gazed at Bur leaning against the wall with his eyes shut, and their faces went still. Then, both elderly women took an arm each and half-carried him, swiftly, easily, through the front door. Edward, who had opened his mouth to explain, left it open in astonishment and the words dried up.

'Upstairs, sister?' said Astrid.

'Upstairs!' said Mae, glowing with excitement. She was dwarfed by Bur's stature, but her small, plump feet were sure on the stairs and she was hardly wheezing at all.

Astrid looked down at Edward, with a flash of her old grimness. 'Wait in the downstairs room!'

He hesitated as Bur was borne rapidly out of sight, then reluctantly obeyed.

The room at the end of the hall seemed darker and more full of sea-sound than ever. He wasn't sure he wanted to be in here by himself. He went in slowly, past Mae's armchair with the jigsaw lying on the side table nearby. She'd put in some more pieces: the picture was of a vast tree, its branches spreading as far as the three corners she'd filled in already.

There was a strong, salty smell in his nostrils but the tiny window wasn't open. The pane was so cloudy he couldn't see the garden through it: all he could see was a sort of bleached fog. As he looked out, he was uneasily conscious of the glass-eye paperweight watching his back from the mantelpiece. It seemed to draw him to it, and he felt compelled to pick it up. In his hand it was malleable and almost warm. He put it back hastily, with a shudder of disgust.

'We were given the eye,' came a whisper behind him, 'by the All-Father, though it didn't do him much good. We don't need eyes. Our seeing is done in different ways.'

Zelma must have been sitting in her armchair, quiet as a ghost, all the time he'd been in the room; it was hard to see her against the faded chintz chair covering.

'I'm sorry . . .'

'There's nothing to be sorry about. You've done the right thing.'

He realized she was talking about Bur. She must have heard them come into the hall. 'You mean it was OK to bring him here?'

'We were expecting a guest.'

'But do you know who Bur is? He's—'

'I know.'

A radiance seemed to hang in the room as Astrid and Mae came in; the dark corners brightened as if the two old women reflected light. Neither sister seemed out of breath after lugging a heavy young man up the stairs.

Mae's plump fingers patted Edward. 'We've settled him in bed. Good boy, bringing him here.'

'But I left his father's message at home,' said Edward guiltily. 'I haven't given it to him yet.'

'Well, it's not the right time now!' said Astrid.

Edward bit his lip and turned to Mae for support. 'Locke's hunting him, you know. He must want the message!'

The old women exchanged quick glances he didn't understand. 'Do you have any information yet, sister?' Mae asked Astrid.

Asrid closed her eyes briefly, then shook her head in irritation. 'I can't see. It's too recent. Your time still, I think.'

'Shall I look, then?' Mae looked at Zelma eagerly, as if for permission, then stood still, screwing up her eyes like a small child playing a game. After a few seconds, she blinked uncertainly. Her pink and white cheeks had paled. She quavered, 'He's lost his boat, sisters. It's happened as you said it would, Zelma.'

The three sisters turned stricken faces to each other. Mae and Astrid went to stand beside Zelma's chair, each taking one of her wrinkled hands. Shadows seemed to drift from the corners and gather about the little group.

'Losing his boat? Is that so bad?' said Edward at last, into the cold, dark silence.

It was Zelma who answered, mad Zelma, whispering from her chair. 'To Bur, as you call him, to him and his kind a boat is as precious as a soul. In losing his boat he's lost himself. Lost, away from his people, in a place of strangeness to him.'

'I thought I saw his soul – floating in time – rudderless in a dark sea,' whispered Mae fearfully.

'What does that mean?' Edward said, baffled.

'In simple terms, he can't get home until he finds his boat,' Astrid said.

'And how can he find it now?' wailed Mae.

'He can't, of course,' said Astrid. 'He'll need help.'

She was looking pointedly at Edward as she spoke, and so, he realized, were the other two sisters. Even Zelma's faded eyes had focused on him.

'My help?' he said apprehensively. Hadn't he done enough already?

'The boat's somewhere in Uffenham,' said Mae. 'I sense it here. That's why he's come, of course.' She shut her eyes for a moment, then left Zelma and sagged into her armchair. 'It's no good. I can't see enough yet.'

Astrid fixed Edward with an accusing eye, as if it was his fault. She was still holding Zelma's hand protectively. 'But I don't see what I can do,' he said.

'Find the boat, of course!'

'Why me?'

'Why you?' she growled. 'Isn't it obvious? He's upstairs in bed, and won't get better until it's found, we're far too old for that sort of gallivanting around, but you're fit and active.'

Edward's heart sank. He looked at them: Astrid, standing there in her scrawny witchlike way; little Mae, plump and asthmatic; and Zelma, frail enough for the wind to blow through her. Three mad old sisters. Why on earth had he brought Bur here? What had he got himself into when he took that message? And now, a lost boat. How could you lose a boat?

'There must be some other way for Bur to get home,' he said in disbelief. 'Where does he live, anyway?'

'Sometimes there's only one way of reaching places,' whispered Zelma, in her gentle, dreamy voice. 'If you want to enter a room, you've first to open the right door. There's only one door to the place where Bur comes from. It can only be reached by sea.'

'And he can only return in his own boat,' said Mae.

'There's his father, that old man,' said Edward. 'Why can't he contact the boatyards here?'

'He's far away, that's why.'

'But where Bur comes from can't be far away. He can't have swum from there! He must be staying somewhere here, maybe further up the coast.'

Mae shook her white head from side to side so that her hair floated like candy floss. 'All the way across the sea, child.'

'Across the ice-bright sea,' murmured Zelma, staring through the window. In spite of himself Edward turned to look, as if she might have suddenly seen beyond the cloudy glass his own dream island, imprisoned in a frozen sea.

'Look,' he said, as firmly as he could, 'I'll go and

get the message. Maybe it'll help Bur solve his boat problem.'

They made no move to stop him going. As usual it was Mae who showed him out. 'Not frightened, are you?' she said, peering up at him solemnly, as she opened the front door.

'Of course not. I know Bur's safe with you.'

It was the wrong answer. She shook her head, disappointed. 'You've got to be strong, you know.'

'I'm not looking for the boat if that's what you mean. I'm on holiday! I've got better things to do.'

But yes, he was frightened, he thought. Frightened of being snared in the strange, enchanted world of the Newnes sisters and of not being able to escape.

He didn't look back until he had crossed the little cobbled yard. She hadn't shut the front door yet, and he could see her looking after him, her white hand raised in the darkness of the hall. But whether it was raised in farewell or supplication, begging for his help, he didn't know.

CHAPTER SEVEN

Wolf

His jacket, rather damp, was back on the hall peg in Gull Cottage, and the piece of paper safely in the pocket. He transferred it at once to his jeans, pushing it well down the pocket in the right leg. The pocket on the other side was still full of half-eaten roll.

He was about to go straight out again, when Fen came out of the kitchen. 'Where are you off to? It's suppertime!'

'Already?' he said, startled. He hadn't realized so much time had passed.

'And where's Matt?'

'He's with Vali. I guess he won't want supper.' Matt was probably going to be with Vali a lot these holidays, thought Edward, and a pang went through him.

Through the open door of the sitting-room his uncle rustled his newspaper crossly. 'He must let us know in future. He can't use this place like a hotel!'

'A five-star hotel, of course.' Fen winked at Edward. 'I've made a breakfast picnic for tomorrow. Did you ask Daniel to come with us?'

'Forgot all about it. Sorry.' It was true that it had gone completely out of his head, but in any case he couldn't face Daniel. Daniel belonged to a different, happier, time.

'You should bring a friend to supper sometime,' said Uncle Hodder from his chair, eyeing him over the top of his reading glasses. 'Fen and I wouldn't mind, we'd like it.'

'Maybe,' he said. 'Thanks, anyway.'

He swallowed his helping of casserole as fast as possible and gave them some cursory help with the washing up, while outside the sun stained the sky with red and sank slowly into the sea. Then he rushed upstairs to fetch a warmer top.

There was a knock at the door as he pulled on his hoodie and Uncle Hodder, looking oddly shy, came in holding a large book under his arm. He thrust it awkwardly at Edward. 'Came across this the other day in one of my lots. I'd meant to keep it for your birthday, but I thought you might like it now.'

It was a collection of the drawings of Leonardo da Vinci, bound in battered leather with a narrow gold trim, and each page separated by brown tissue paper fragile as moths' wings.

Edward turned the pages reverently. 'But this is amazing! Are you sure—' He looked up anxiously. 'Are you sure you shouldn't sell it?'

His uncle was smiling as he watched him. It was a proper smile, the first Edward had seen him give since he and Matt had arrived, and it spread to his eyes. 'Quite sure I'm sure. Fen's always going on about how much you can learn from the great artists, and he's surely one of the greatest. Anyway, what are nephews for if not to give things to occasionally? Take care of it. It's valuable.'

'Thanks, I will. You bet!' If it had been Dad and not Uncle Hodder he might have flung his arms round him; it was such a *right* sort of present. But there was still an invisible barrier between them. He saw that his uncle felt it too, for though he went on smiling, it grew sad. 'Don't be too lonely, Edward.'

He pretended to study one of the drawings. 'What d'you mean?'

'Don't seal yourself away. It's so easy. I've done it myself.' He hesitated. 'We still have each other, we mustn't forget that. We must get to know each other properly now. I know I can't take your father's place, but I'd like to do more for you and Matt.'

Edward kept his eyes glued to his book. His heart beat sickeningly slowly. He had heard the note of uncertainty, of pleading in his uncle's voice but he wasn't going to help him out, he couldn't. There was an endless silence while his uncle waited for some sign from him. Then at last the door shut and he was alone.

A quick look at the drawings, then he'd set out again.

Dusk was falling outside when he put the book down. He glanced over at the window as he left the room. A round moon was high in the sky, and beneath it the sea gleamed like a sheet of ice.

Across the ice-bright sea.

It was there again! All the narrow window could show him was just a little bit of land, but its shadow stretched across the water from the silver horizon. The land, the island, whatever it was, was back, and this time he knew it wasn't just his imagination.

He turned and ran through the door, down the stairs, out of the front door. The ten o'clock news on television covered the thump of his feet.

The air outside was damp, not cold. He tore through from the High Street into Marine Street, down one of the alleyways and on to the Parade. There he stopped, gasping for breath.

The Parade and the spread of moonlit shingle in front of him were deserted. There was no wind. Under the great blue-black arch of the sky the sea was unmoving. Far off, a shape floated over its flat surface and rose up to touch the stars.

Land! thought Edward. *It is! It is!* He ran to the

low wall on the other side of the Parade and leaned against it, staring into the moonlight. The moon threw a silver road down across the sea. It looked so solid he imagined walking along it all the way to the island to find his father; or his father walking along it back to him. 'Dad?' he whispered into the huge silence before him. 'Dad? Are you out there?'

'You all right, young man?' said a voice close by.

It was a large man buttoned into a mackintosh, taking a small, woolly-looking dog for a walk.

'Can you see it?' Edward asked breathlessly.

The man peered at him. 'What are you on about?'

'That island, over there. Can you see it?' He pointed to the horizon, and turned to the man expectantly.

'I see a cloud. Is that what you mean?'

'It's land! It's an island!'

The man gave him a wary look. 'Could well be. I haven't got my glasses on me right now. They're back at the hotel, and that's where we're off to, Sandy and me. Come along, Sandy! Mother's waiting.' And with a tug on the small dog's lead, he was gone.

Edward stood alone, while the man's footsteps died away. He stared at the shape on the horizon, and extraordinary possibilities shimmered in his head. There was no time to waste. He turned from the sea abruptly, went back into Marine Street and began to jog towards Neptune Alley.

The curtains were drawn in the little cottages. The residents of Uffenham had had their suppers and would be thinking about retiring to bed; the two hotels on the Parade would be full of guests drinking coffee after their posh dinners and looking out of the lounge windows at the quiet, moonlit sea. Perhaps they'd see the island and think it was just a cloud.

He jogged on past the cottages. Now he could see the entrance to Neptune Alley. He slowed down and turned into it.

There were no lights down here. Its high walls threw the way between into shadow, but through the archway halfway down he could see the Newneses' cottage gleaming in the moonlight as if it stood in snow.

Then something ran across the archway on his side, something that wasn't a shadow.

Edward stepped nearer, uncertainly. The thing moved out of the shadows and stood there in the moonlight in front of the archway. It was a dog, an Alsatian. It had seen him. Its ears were pricked and he saw the pale gleam of its eyes.

He liked dogs. He wasn't nervous. He moved closer to the archway and the waiting dog, murmuring softly. 'Good dog, good boy.'

The dog growled, long and low, a warning growl. It pulled its black lips back and its sharp, pointed teeth were clearly visible. It meant business. It was not going to allow him to get through to the Newneses' cottage.

He stopped, puzzled. The old ladies didn't own a dog. It must be a stray. 'What are you up to, then, boy?' he whispered softly.

It stood still, watching him, its body tense and quivering slightly, four legs planted in the centre of the archway. The moonlight brindled its coat and made a silver ridge of its hackles.

He moved forward a little, to the right side of the archway. The dog snarled again, its eyes fixed on him. It wasn't going to attack him unless he actually went past it. But he wanted to go past it, he had to get past it.

It might be tamed by food.

Edward stood still. His hand crept to his left-hand pocket, pulled out the remains of the bread roll, now dry and hard. 'Good boy. Look what I've got.'

He showed the dog. Its nostrils dilated. He stepped closer until he could feel the archway brush his shoulder. He put one foot over the invisible line the dog had drawn, still holding the bread in his hand.

The dog leapt. Edward shouted something, he wasn't sure what, and threw the bread at the dog; and the dog, the bread in its mouth, its eyes rolling horribly, seemed to fall back and be swallowed by shadow. Then Edward was through the archway and stumbling towards the front door of the cottage, throwing himself against it without looking back. The door was opened rapidly by someone on the other side and he fell over the threshold.

'Well done. We've been expecting you.'

With a click the door closed behind him. Astrid was standing there in a thin grey dressing-gown, and looking at him almost approvingly.

'You've got a guard dog out there!' said Edward. His legs were trembling.

'We don't need guards. What did you use?'

'Use? I threw it some bread, if that's what you mean.'

'Bread? Excellent protection against the supernatural.' She gazed at him strangely, a look which held pity, yet hope. The dressing-gown had softened her fierce outline. 'The dog, as you call it, was one of *his* creatures. He has three to use against you, the man who calls himself Locke. That was only the first.'

She was crazy, wasn't she? Edward touched the paper in his pocket to reassure himself, and looked up the dimly-lit stairs. 'I've brought the message. I'll take it to Bur now.'

'No, you won't.' Astrid gripped his arm. 'Didn't I tell you it wasn't the right time? He's asleep.'

Then Mae materialized at his other side. 'Come

and sit down, dear,' she said soothingly. 'You've had a shock.'

Before he could protest, Edward found himself being guided down the hall to the small back room. The curtains weren't drawn, and bright moonlight was diffused through the cloudy pane, though a standard lamp had been switched on over the table with the jigsaw.

Mae sat down and patted the chair opposite her invitingly. She was wearing a pair of glasses with sparkly, winged frames and a dressing-gown, newer and brighter than her sister's, knitted from fluffy, pale-yellow wool. She resembled a plump and overgrown chick, and the glasses gave the outfit a jaunty air. The smile she gave Edward was equally cheery, though gummy. She must have taken her teeth out for the night.

'Where's Zelma?' said Edward shakily, finding he was glad to sit down.

'In bed, dear. She's a little overtired. All the excitement, you know.' She leaned forward gleefully. 'So Locke's wolf didn't defeat you!'

He took a deep breath to steady himself. 'Look, I want to make a bargain with you.'

'A bargain?'

'I'll find the boat,' he said, 'if Bur takes me back with him when I've found it – to wherever he's come from.' He saw the exchange of startled glances between the old women, and added quickly, 'For a visit, I mean, that's all.'

Was it such a big thing to ask? But they both looked most put out, even alarmed. Mae drew her mouth down beneath the sparkly glasses. In the draining silver light she looked suddenly ugly and frightened, the plump pouches in her cheeks turning to hollows without her dentures. 'I'm not sure it's possible, dear.'

An immense longing overwhelmed him. He saw again the magical island floating on the horizon; he imagined sailing there with Bur to rescue Dad. He could feel Dad's arms around him and hear his whispered words of love. But when he blinked he could only see Astrid's face, the bones showing hard and implacable beneath the grey papery skin.

Mae said tremulously into the silence, 'Should I fetch Zelma?'

'I think we should take the responsibility for this,' Astrid said thoughtfully at last. 'I don't see why Zelma has to make all the decisions.' Her fierce gaze rested on Edward. 'You must wait a while for your answer.'

'Without Zelma here?' wailed Mae, and she twisted her little hands together. 'Oh, Astrid, I can't see what will happen so far ahead, and neither can you!'

'We can't always depend on Zelma,' said Astrid tightly. She sniffed. 'I have my own gift, different from Zelma's, I agree, but it has its uses. Even if the pattern changes, the outcome must surely be the same. Let us listen and see.' She held up a knobbly hand, quelling Mae's protests.

Edward sat and waited, his heart beating fast in hope, though he didn't know what was going to happen; and suddenly he heard a high murmuring in the room that wasn't the deep sea-sound he recognized, but like a wind. Astrid and Mae cocked their heads to it, and the silver light from the window gleamed in their eyes.

When at last it died away, Mae quavered, 'But it didn't tell us anything new, Astrid! Only the elements of the pattern.'

Astrid ignored her and turned to Edward. 'You can have your bargain, boy. When you find the boat you may sail with the young man you call Bur.'

Mae's mouth fell open in dismay. 'What have you promised, Astrid? You realize what that means?'

She nodded brusquely. 'He'll have to return the boy here before he leaves for good.'

'But think of the danger!'

'It's a risk we have to take. Anyway, Zelma will realize we have no choice. We're in desperate need of the boy's help.'

'I know, sister,' whispered Mae, but she still looked frightened.

'I'll do my best,' Edward said eagerly. He tried

to think of some sensible questions before Astrid changed her mind. 'Do you know anything about this boat? If it's a sailing boat, how big is it? Do you know what make it is?'

'All we can tell you is that she's called *Ringhorn*,' Mae said. The name rippled round the room like water.

'Of course we can't tell you what she looks like,' said Astrid. 'It's years since we've seen her. We've lived in your time too long.'

'But I can't go round searching every boat in Uffenham for one that's called *Ringhorn*. It's impossible!'

Astrid eyed him grimly. 'Use courage and wit, boy. You've proved you possess courage tonight.'

'But how did Bur lose his boat in the first place? I mean – it's a big thing to lose!' He looked at the old women with a half-smile, but their faces were sombre.

'She's not lost in that sense, foolish boy!' said Astrid.

'He doesn't understand,' Mae said softly. 'Let me tell him how it happened. Let me look again.' She heaved herself out of her chair and drew herself up stiffly in the moonlight, looking as if she were about to recite a party piece; a small, dignified figure in spite of the fluffy dressing-gown. 'It's coming,' she said after a moment. 'I see light on water, fish shining in a net. Now there's sand – a cove, I think.'

As Edward listened in bewilderment, her voice was unchanged: chatty and slightly breathless, as if what she was doing was perfectly normal. 'I see our boy now – he's pulled *Ringhorn* up the beach. There's a drift of woodsmoke on the air. He's made a fire to cook a meal.' She stopped a moment and gave a little gasp, and the moonlight shifted on the window pane, making the room suddenly darker.

'The Trickster's there, waiting. There's wind and darkness and the Trickster's in the middle of it. He blows *Ringhorn* away from shore, and our poor boy – oh, dear – he's plunged into the sea after her! I see him tossed in the water, the waves are carrying him, carrying him far . . .'

As Edward stared at her, Mae gave a final wheeze and sat down with a thump, flashing a triumphant look at Astrid. 'There! It was clearer this time. But at the end I couldn't see beyond the spray.'

'You mean, that was what actually happened?' said Edward, bemused. 'But how could you see it like that?'

Mae gave a modest smile. 'It's my gift, dear.'

'So Bur tried to *swim* after his boat?' he said incredulously.

'Locke knew Bur would follow her, whatever it cost him,' she said, sighing.

'And it was Locke who stole the boat?'

Astrid grunted with impatience. 'Do you need everything explained? Locke, as he's calling himself, is also known by us as the Trickster. He's an expert in the art of deception and disguises. And he hates Bur. He's stolen *Ringhorn* to put Bur's life in danger.'

'But how could he hide himself in a puff of wind? I don't understand.'

'Do you understand everything in your own world?'

'But why does he hate Bur so much?' said Edward doggedly. 'I mean, they're relations . . .'

She laughed dourly. 'Can you really know so little?'

'Let me explain,' said Mae. 'Locke wasn't always like this, you see.' She settled herself more comfortably and took off her glasses, admiring the way they glittered in the moonlight.

'Once upon a time Bur's father looked on him as a brother. He was such an attractive, vibrant young man. That hair, those smiling eyes! Everyone thought him so amusing and clever, didn't they, Astrid? He was a great one for the ladies.' She patted her candy floss hair coyly, and gave a reflective sigh. 'They loved him, the ladies did. He was the life and soul of every party, and he had his party tricks. That was before the tricks got out of hand.'

'Tricks?'

'Tricks – pranks – jokes – they started getting malicious. They weren't funny any more, they were nasty, evil, they hurt people. It all began as soon as Bur was born. He was the one his father favoured. His father knew he was special, and he was. From the very beginning it was clear that Bur and Locke were as different as sunlight and shadow.'

'So Locke's always been jealous of Bur?'

'You haven't understood at all!' said Astrid sharply. 'Don't you see that they were born to try and cancel the other out? Cruelty and compassion, hurt and healing, life and death – it's the story of all such things.'

He turned to Mae helplessly. She leaned forward and patted his knee. 'Never mind, dearie. Watch out for Locke, that's all. He won't want you finding that boat.'

A thought struck him. 'But you must know what it looks like! You've just seen what happened!'

Her glance slid away from him and she looked suddenly secretive. 'I don't remember, child. The pictures fade too fast.' She pushed herself up, wheezing noisily with the effort, and held out an arm to him for help. He took it reluctantly, knowing it was a deliberate ploy to stop him asking more.

'But the message! Can't I see Bur?'

'It's late, dear, too late for old women like us. Bring it back another time. We must prepare ourselves for the night, and you . . .' she looked up at him with a toothless grin, as if she had achieved just what she wanted, '. . . *you* must prepare yourself for the finding!'

CHAPTER EIGHT

Murder Weapon

There was no sign of the animal, whatever it was, in the deserted alleyway. Edward cut through to the Parade to look at the horizon on his way home. The moon hung over an empty sea. The island had disappeared. But he'd seen it twice now. He knew it was there. It was the other half of the bargain and it was there somewhere, waiting for him.

The night had remained fine and mild, and the Parade was busier than it had been earlier. The two hotels were brightly lit and some of the guests were coming out to enjoy a walk before bed. Further along, in front of the Cross Keys, couples were sitting on the wall to look at the moon and finish their drinks. He recognized Matt and Vali as he came closer. They were arguing. Matt sounded belligerent, as if he'd had too much to drink and had got beyond the being-funny stage.

He turned as Edward came up, and gave him a crazy grin. 'Hi, little guy!' His voice was slurred. 'Let's go home. Just have some sleep first.' He lurched against Vali and closed his eyes.

Vali looked at Edward with relief over the top of Matt's head. 'We must take Matt home, Edward. He has been saying such things about your uncle—'

Edward's heart sank. 'He doesn't mean them. How's he got like this?' He'd never seen Matt drunk before, never.

'It was one of the boys, the one from the beach. I like him at first . . .' she shrugged, '. . . but now, I don't know. He keep bringing Matt drinks – beer, wine – because Matt, he must not go in the bar. Matt keep drinking them and this Wolf, he keep bringing out more.'

'Wolf?' said Edward uneasily.

'That is his name. How you call it, nickname, I think?'

'Well, he's made him drunk! Matt, wake up!'

Matt opened his eyes. He smiled wickedly. 'I've got something of yours, Ed. Told you to throw it away, didn't I? Now I've confiscated it.' He opened his palm. In it lay Edward's stone.

Edward stared indignantly. 'Give it here!' He leaned forward and grabbed it before Matt's slowed reactions could prevent him. 'You took it today, didn't you? You thief!'

Matt seemed to flop. He looked at his hand, smeared with new blood. 'It's sharp,' he murmured in apparent surprise.

Edward swallowed his anger. Vali hoisted Matt to his feet with her usual awesome strength and frogmarched him off, with Edward hurrying along on his other side, holding the stone gingerly. By the time they reached the High Street, Matt seemed to have sobered up a little. He walked more or less by himself to the front door of Gull Cottage.

' 'Night,' he said with great dignity to Vali.

Edward took the spare key from Matt's pocket and opened the door. The cottage was in darkness. Fen and Uncle Hodder had gone to bed. He pushed Matt up the stairs as quietly as possible, but Matt didn't need much help. When they reached the back bedroom, Matt threw himself down on his bed and pulled up the duvet.

'Sorry, Ed,' he said contritely. Then he closed his eyes and fell fast asleep, still fully dressed in his sweatshirt and jeans.

Edward looked at the stone in his hand. A new hiding place, safe from Matt? He'd find one in the morning. In the meantime, Matt didn't look as if he was capable of moving. He pulled open the drawer of the chest and put the stone back in. There was no point in wrapping it up to hide it any longer, and anyway his T-shirt was useless. The stone had cut it to shreds.

Edward swum up through a deep pool of sleep and was aware that something had woken him. The night seemed silent; the sea too calm to hear. When he opened his eyes the room was in darkness, but through the dark a darker shape moved soundlessly. It passed by the foot of his bed and went towards the door. Matt, going to the loo.

The door was opened and a shaft of light from the landing sliced across the floorboards. Matt moved through the light, one hand outstretched like a sleepwalker's, and in his hand something glinted.

Edward came fully awake. He sat up, rubbing his eyes. The chest drawer was open. Full of foreboding, he leapt out of bed.

'*What are you doing with my stone?*'

It was a furious whisper, but Matt didn't stop. Instead he moved on, robot-like, across the tiny landing. Slowly and with dreadful determination, he passed the bathroom and the boxroom until he was outside the door of the bedroom Uncle Hodder and Fen shared; and in his hand the stone gleamed as sharp and cold as a dagger blade.

'Matt! For God's sake—'

Edward shot across the landing and grabbed a handful of Matt's sweatshirt. Matt was taller and stronger and he found he had to clench both arms round him to keep him stationary. For the next few seconds an intense silent struggle took place on the landing: Matt determined to move forward; Edward desperate to stop him. At last Edward managed to grip Matt's wrist and squeeze. Strength must have come to him from somewhere, for suddenly Matt's hand went limp and the stone dropped, dropped with a dull thud on to the bare boards of the landing.

They faced each other, the stone lying between them. Edward was panting, but Matt breathed normally. He looked normal now too, though slightly puzzled. As Edward tried to speak, he held his finger to his lips and nodded behind him at the bedroom door. 'Shh! We mustn't wake them. What are you up to out here?'

'What are *you* up to?' demanded Edward.

Matt ran his fingers through his fair hair in a bewildered way so that it stuck up like feathers. 'Going to the bathroom, I think. You'd better join the queue.'

'That's not true! You were—' But what he thought Matt was going to do was too horrible to put into words.

Matt suddenly looked extremely pale. 'I feel sick!' he said in astonishment, and the next moment he had vanished into the bathroom.

Edward tried not to listen to what was going on

inside. He bent down and picked the stone up cautiously between his thumb and forefinger. Back in the bedroom he wrapped it in the ragged strips of T-shirt and put the bundle into the small backpack that held his sketching things.

It was the most beautiful and unusual stone he'd ever found. But beautiful and unusual as it was, he'd have to get rid of it in the morning. Matt had been drunk; he hadn't known what he was doing. Sharp as a weapon, he'd said about the stone, and it was as a weapon that he'd been going to use it.

Yes, it was just too dangerous to keep.

CHAPTER NINE

Hide and Seek

Fen had to wake Edward the next morning. 'Come on, sleepyhead! Have you forgotten we're off sketching? Don't wake Matt.'

'Not much chance of that!' Edward looked enviously at Matt's unstirring shape beneath the duvet. He felt thick and heavy, as if he had the hangover, not Matt.

As he pulled on his jeans the paper in the pocket rustled. He should be delivering the message to Bur and starting the search for the boat, not wasting time sketching. At least he could get rid of the stone while he was out.

By the time they reached the marshes, he felt better. The sun was warm on his face; his hoodie prickled his neck. Fen strode straight to her favourite spot, where two dykes joined in a right angle, making a wall to the curve of the river on one side and the long dyke ditch, filled with dark green water, on the other.

Edward panted up the slope of the dyke after her. The backs of her bare legs under the faded denim sack she called her sketching skirt were all stringy muscle, like sea-salty rope. The legs and the skirt cut a swathe through the long, coarse grass, until at the top she sat down with a triumphant thump. 'Let's see what we can make of this!'

Edward sat well away; he knew Fen hated to be cramped when she was working. He pulled off his hoodie and, in a half-hearted way, set about planning his sketch.

It was a good spot for sketching. The river stretched away before him, clear, clean and empty in the morning light. Seagulls wheeled in the sky above them; a few boats lay at their moorings to the left. Further left still, the yacht club and the two slipways broke the bend of the river, with the dark stump of the Martello tower standing guard on the sea wall. In the foreground immediately below him lay an ancient rowing-boat, mostly submerged by water and surrounded by spindly moorhens pecking busily at the tidemark.

It was when Edward dug out his pad and pencil box from the backpack that he saw the stone. It must have been jolted out of its wrappings during the walk. He gazed down at it, astonished again by its beauty as sunlight flickered through it, lighting a cold green fire in its heart. He'd carry it with him a little longer, but keep it well away from Matt. He pushed the stone back inside his backpack and began to sketch.

'How's it going?' Fen called over, after what seemed a very long time.

'Badly.' He couldn't still his mind enough for the lines and shapes and shadows to enter and take over. He couldn't think about anything except reaching the island.

'Never mind. Fancy an egg and bacon roll?'

She hadn't been sketching the river at all, but a clump of grasses with some tall purple daisies sticking out of them.

'That's brilliant!'

'Thanks.' Fen looked modest, but a pleased smile tweaked her lips. '*Aster tripolium*, commonly known as sea aster. Let's have some breakfast.'

They ate, staring out across the river. Edward, his thoughts in a whirl, jumped when Fen said casually, 'Get any nightmares these days?'

'Why d'you ask?'

'Maybe I associate them with egg and bacon. Remember how you used to tell us your dreams at breakfast? I never knew if you'd really had them, or made them up to spoil our appetites!'

'They were true. Dad managed to stop them in the end.'

'How?' Fen squinted at him against the sun.

'He'd say, "It's just a nightmare running away with you. Take the reins. You can control it. It's all in your head." It seemed to work when I thought of it like that – like a bolting horse.'

'He was sensible, your dad,' said Fen. 'Never held anything against me for not making an honest man of his brother.'

Her hair was glossy in the sunlight, but Edward saw what he'd never noticed before: that there were grey hairs sparkling amongst the dark, like fine strands of tinsel. Panic caught in his throat. 'You'll always be here in the summer, won't you?'

'For your uncle?'

'For all of us.'

Her strong, lean face suddenly softened. 'Of course. We belong together, Fenella Jones and the Hodders.' She screwed the top back on the Thermos. 'Back to work?'

'Mine's not worth it.' He looked at his sketch ruefully, holding it so she couldn't see, and shook his head. 'I can't draw any more. I've lost it.'

'Nonsense. Drawing needs practice, like anything else. Nothing's ever lost.'

'Dad is,' he said abruptly.

'What?'

'That's what Mae Newnes said.'

'What exactly did she say?' said Fen, puzzled.

'That I'd lost my father.'

'Oh, Edward!' Fen looked as if she didn't know whether to laugh or cry. 'That's what people say when someone's died. It's just a polite way of avoiding the dreaded "d" word. You know it is!'

'I suppose.' He looked away from her, to the distant dazzle of the sea. There was no sign of the island.

'You haven't *lost* your father, anyway,' said Fen. 'He may not be around any more, but he's still your father. Nothing can change that. Your relationship with him will go on developing, though it may be hard to understand that at the moment.'

Edward stood up quickly. He couldn't listen any more. If he did, he might stop believing that Dad was on the island.

'I've got to go. There's something I should be doing. Sorry, Fen.'

She shook her head. 'I'm glad you're busy.'

He slid down the side of the dyke, down the flattened path they had made in the grass on their way up. He looked up to wave as he reached the bottom. Fen was gazing down at him, a small frown between her brows.

The sailing club would be the best place to start searching for *Ringhorn*. At this time of the morning most of the dinghies would still be lying on their trailers, waiting for the day's sail. He could wander along the rows of boats without being disturbed. The problem was the fixed-keel boats dotted about the river on their moorings in front of the club. He wasn't sure how he'd manage to look at those. But perhaps he'd be lucky and find *Ringhorn* amongst the dinghies on the shore. Perhaps he'd find her this morning!

There were few people around yet: a man in overalls scraping the bottom of his boat, a couple of kids he didn't know launching a rowing boat from one of the slipways. All the same, Edward decided to start down at the far end of the boatpark, away from the clubhouse.

He walked by the first few boats. Then he realized with a sinking feeling what a fool he'd been not to remember.

The boats were all under covers – plastic or rubber – but so efficiently and completely covered against the elements that in most cases he'd have to lift or undo the tapes on the covers to see the boat's name. Some names had been painted on the covers, but most hadn't. The search would take for ever.

'What are you doing?'

Halfway along the row, Edward looked up guiltily, though why he should feel guilty, he didn't know. But it was only Lyddie, the sun glinting on her glasses and her freckled face puzzled. She was wearing the same geeky T-shirt over a swimming costume, and her forearms and legs were round and tanned. She looked like a small brown bun.

'I'm looking for something,' he said shortly.

'A boat?'

Brilliant, thought Edward. But he made an effort. 'More of a name, really. I don't know whether she's a Wayfarer or a Lapwing or what, so I've got to look for the right name.'

'Want me to help?' Her face was eager.

'Up to you.'

'I don't mind. What's she called?'

'*Ringhorn*,' he said reluctantly. The name seemed to have its own echo in the air.

She looked doubtfully at the row of dinghies. 'Sounds a bit grand for a Lapwing.'

He shrugged, and she didn't ask any more questions. In fact, although she seemed grateful to Edward for allowing her to do something with him, she was totally tongue-tied.

'You here all holidays?' he asked at last.

'A month.' She undid a clip on a blue plastic cover and added politely, 'What about you?'

'Till the Bank Holiday. Just me and Matt. Mum's not coming. She's working.'

'It's not fair,' Lyddie burst out suddenly. 'Daniel's got a friend staying and I wanted one too, only Mum says there's not room in my bedroom and Daniel asked first.'

Daniel had never had a friend to stay at Uffenham before. He'd always done things with Edward. He hadn't needed anyone else. 'What's this friend like?'

'Terrible. He laughs at me. He makes Daniel laugh at me, too.' Enormous tears welled in her eyes, magnified by the glasses.

'Why does he laugh at you?'

'He says I'm fat. He's called Patrick and he's good at everything. Daniel thinks he's cool.'

Edward undid another clip thoughtfully. 'How long's he staying?'

'Ages.'

It didn't matter anyway, Edward told himself. He'd planned to avoid Daniel these holidays, hadn't he?

It grew hotter as the sun rose in the sky. Edward's palms were sweating and his fingers hurt from undoing so many tapes, toggles and clips. Some of them were so sticky with salt and from being left fastened since last summer that they were almost impossible to undo. On its mound above the boat park the tower looked down on him imperviously.

And now more and more people were arriving. He and Lyddie were getting some odd looks as they made their erratic progress down the rows of boats, but worse, some boats were being hauled away to the slipways before they had a chance to look at their names.

Sea Dancer, *Merlin*, *Gumboot*, *Miss England*, *Ariel* – no sign of a *Ringhorn*. They were using him, the Newnes sisters. They'd set him up to find the boat, with the reward of a visit to the island.

'This is a bit boring,' said Lyddie timidly. The bits round her freckles were pink with heat. 'Shall we do something else? Go swimming? Mum won't mind if I'm with you.'

'I've got to go on looking,' said Edward.

'But why have you? Is it that important?'

'It's . . .' he paused, '. . . life and death important.'

'Really?' In the sun Lyddie's tears had dried to salty runnels on her cheeks and her eyes behind her glasses fastened on him: large, amazed, unexpectedly pretty hazel eyes. 'You're not joking, are you?'

'Would I be slaving away under a hot sun doing this if I was joking?'

'But don't you know who owns her? You could look it up in the sailing club register instead of all this hard work.'

He was impressed by her quick thinking, but tried not to show it. 'It still wouldn't help, not with this boat.'

'Why not?'

'She wouldn't be in it, that's why.'

'Are you sure this boat even exists?'

''Course she does.' He looked at Lyddie's doubtful face and felt his conviction sway dangerously.

'Would it matter if we got a drink?' she asked a little dolefully. 'I'm really thirsty.'

They were on their way to the club when to Edward's surprise he saw Matt, taking the cover off Uncle Hodder's boat. Until now Edward had avoided the row of Wayfarers in which it stood.

Matt looked up and grinned at them. His face looked clear and open, as if it had been purged of its usual dark, angry expression. 'Hi, guys. I thought I'd see what sort of shape *Freya*'s in.'

'You mean you're going sailing?' said Edward in disbelief. He made himself look at *Freya*. She'd been fitted with a new, shiny silver mast and repainted a dark blue. There were new sailbags in the bows. He saw with relief that there was nothing left to show of that dreadful day when she had been found with her mast a broken stalk, her mainsail gone.

'I thought I'd ask Hodder to come out with me this afternoon,' said Matt. 'Get him out of that stuffy old bookshop.' He squinted into the sun, smiling. 'There's not much wind but it's a terrific day. Why don't you come?'

'Thanks, but no thanks,' said Edward. 'How's your hangover?'

'Get off! What hangover? It never happened.'

It had, thought Edward, *and something else*. The memory of the night stirred for a second and darkened the sun.

He ran after Lyddie, up the wooden steps of the clubhouse. In the main room people in darned guernseys and baggy trousers stood by the bar drinking beer and talking loudly and cheerfully about the weekend's races.

'I've got some money,' said Lyddie. 'I'll get us a couple of Cokes.'

Edward shifted from leg to leg on the edge of the crowd, swinging his backpack from one hand. He wanted to get back to the search. Lyddie was standing next to a man who had his back to him. He glanced at the man, then looked again.

Wiry build. Short auburn hair that seemed to bristle and quiver with energy. Clothes that didn't look quite right: too new, too carefully chosen. And the hand holding a glass of white wine would be hot if it touched you, burningly hot.

Locke hadn't seen him. As Edward stood mesmerized, he turned and with his easy stride went over to the picture window, the one that looked out on the rows of parked boats. Had he watched Edward search all morning?

Edward grabbed at Lyddie, almost making her drop the two cans of Coke. 'Get out, quick!' he hissed in her ear.

'Why? What's the matter?'

He dragged her away with such force she almost fell over. She ran with Edward past the changing rooms, then through the door and outside.

'What's happened?'

'I'll explain in a minute. Come *on*!'

They thudded down the steps, Edward almost falling, Lyddie following in bewilderment, then charged through the car park and up the steps to the top of the sea wall. There Edward slowed to a walk, his chest heaving, and took one of the cans from Lyddie, but he was panting too much to drink it.

'There was a man in there – I don't want him to know I'm looking for *Ringhorn*!'

Lyddie drew in a deep breath. 'You mean he's – like – the enemy?'

'Right first time. I'm going to have to search somewhere else for a bit, somewhere *he* won't be.' *But perhaps Locke would follow him wherever he searched*, Edward thought uneasily.

Lyddie looked up at him with her big, begging eyes. 'Can I help you some more?'

Suddenly he wanted to be on his own, to think. He pushed the unopened Coke can into his backpack. 'Sorry. It's best I do it myself.'

They began to walk in the direction of Uffenham without speaking to each other, Lyddie burying her face in her can. A warm wind came from nowhere and lifted their hair.

Lyddie was right, Edward thought, Ringhorn *was*

too grand a name for a dinghy. He'd already begun to think of her as a 'she', with a character of her own. She'd have beauty and grace, yet be strongly built to ride the storms and the tossing swell: a true and noble companion for heroic adventure. He'd be more likely to find her among the larger fishing boats pulled up on the beach, or in the boatyard along the grit road back into Uffenham, than here at the sailing club.

The breeze was growing stronger. When he looked up it was to see the sky filling with clouds, the brilliant sun grown hazy.

He stared over the sea. Far out, further than the yachts, their sails blown sideways like scraps of paper in the breeze, where the line of the horizon had blurred into sky and clouds had spread down to touch it, something solid grew up from the sea. Something glistened under the white sky and its form had shadow.

'Look!' He gripped Lyddie. 'D'you see it?'

'Ow! What?'

'Over there!' He dropped her arm. 'Don't bother looking. I forgot about your eyesight.'

'With my glasses on, I can probably see further than you,' she said, with surprising spirit. 'What am I meant to be looking at?'

'Land! See?'

'It's a cloud. What's happened to *your* eyesight?'

It was land, Edward thought, and soon, soon, he would visit it.

He dug his hands into his pockets and the scrap of paper touched his fingertips. He'd go and see Bur now with the message. Perhaps that one word would help in the search.

He walked on rapidly, along the sea wall into Uffenham, leaving Lyddie behind, and the glittering shape on the horizon that was the island stayed with him all the way.

CHAPTER TEN

The Killing Stone

The door to the cottage opened when Edward leaned against it. As he ran swiftly up the stairs the sound of the sea seemed to roar in his head. Without knocking, he pushed the open door to the guest room, then stopped.

The curtains were drawn, and the room was dim and chilly after the heat outside. Bur lay in the bed like a toppled statue, his head turned away on the pillow, one arm outside the bedclothes. As Edward stared in, only the dust stirred around the door.

He took a step towards the bed. 'Bur?'

No answer.

'I need your help,' he said softly. 'I've seen an island far away. That's where you come from, isn't it?' The figure was motionless beneath the faded quilt. He raised his voice. 'You've got to help me if you want me to find your boat!'

He pulled the message from his pocket and waved the crumpled paper before Bur's closed eyes. 'Does this say where *Ringhorn* is?'

At the name the air in the room seemed to shift. The roaring in Edward's head grew louder, as if, impossibly, the sea outside was battering at the cottage walls.

'Wake up! Please wake up!' He touched Bur's arm. It was deathly cold.

In horror he started back from the bed, and at that same moment Mae's little fingers gripped him like steel. 'The message won't help him at the moment. Put it away.'

'Let go of me!' cried Edward. 'He's dead, isn't he?'

Mae was puffing alarmingly and had to sit down on the edge of the bed, still hanging on to him. 'Not dead – but sleeping.'

'Sleeping?'

'Not sleeping as you'd understand it. He's somewhere apart. Waiting.' Seeing Edward's blank face she added, 'He'll be himself when *Ringhorn* is found.'

'But what happens if I don't find her?' said Edward, appalled.

'Not so loud,' said Mae gently. 'My dear boy, you will find her, Zelma's told us so.'

'Did she tell you where?' he said bitterly, shoving the message back in his pocket.

'Come along downstairs now. It's dangerous to disturb him, and anyway, you're beside yourself.' She gave a quick glance beyond him as if expecting to see the other polite, amenable Edward standing alongside. Then, heaving herself up from the bed and leaning on him, she propelled him from the room.

No sunlight came through the little cloudy window of the back room. Mae flopped into her armchair breathing heavily, and Edward took off his backpack and sat opposite. He felt too exhausted and thirsty to speak. He lifted his backpack on to his knees and unbuckled it while Mae watched inquisitively.

'That's a nice shopping bag, dear.'

He put the Coke can to his lips and drank, ignoring her. After a while he relented. 'Where are your sisters?'

'Astrid's out on her business,' she said vaguely, peering at her jigsaw. 'And Zelma's resting upstairs. She tires easily. It's the burden of knowing so much.'

'What does Zelma know?' he said suspiciously.

'What has happened and what will happen again.' Mae paused and her mouth trembled. 'She says we should never have agreed to let you visit the island. She says she can't control what will happen now the pattern's been distorted.'

'But it was a promise!' said Edward, in

consternation. 'You've got to keep your side of the bargain!'

She nodded at him, with a little petulant sigh. 'She shouldn't blame me. It was Astrid's fault too. We don't have Zelma's gifts, but I do what I can in the here and now. Astrid's sometimes a little jealous of me, I'm afraid.' She fitted another piece of jigsaw and surveyed the result complacently.

Frowning, Edward pushed the empty Coke can into his backpack. It dislodged the stone and before he could stop it, it had fallen on to the threadbare carpet. Mae stared down, one plump white hand quivering at her mouth.

'Sorry,' said Edward. He bent down and held the stone out to her. It glowed green against the pink flesh of his palm, the dangerous end pointing away. 'I found it on the beach. Amazing, isn't it?'

She seemed to pale and shrink before his eyes, a tiny old lady clinging to the arms of her chair. He could see where she had dabbed clumsy patches of rouge on her cheeks. 'Get rid of it!' she whispered. 'It doesn't come from the beach, nor from the sea, but from the earth long ago.'

'The earth long ago?' he repeated stupidly. But he had found it in the sand, by the sea's edge.

'It's the mistletoe stone. From time to time it comes into the Trickster's possession.' She added, louder, ominously. 'He'll want to find it.'

Edward stared at her apprehensively. 'The Trickster? You mean Locke, don't you?'

She nodded, and crouched forward. 'Where did you find it? Tell me exactly.'

He thought back, and a little chill crept through him. 'It was where Locke had been walking – in his footprints.'

'It's the killing stone. This time he must have dropped it before he could use it. Get rid of it! Get rid of it so Locke can never find it again!' She began to keen to herself, rocking backwards and forwards on the chair. 'Throw it to the wind! Drop it in the deepest ocean!'

Alarmed, he grabbed the backpack, stood up, and still clutching the stone, backed towards the door.

'Dig a pit for it, deep as hell, and never, never tell!' The sound of the sea rose in his ears, and her voice was a part of it, rising like a wave, flooding the hall and pushing him out of the front door. 'Dig a pit for it, deep as hell, and never, never tell!'

Edward headed for the back streets furthest away from the Parade and the High Street, scared that Locke might suddenly confront him as he had done yesterday. The breeze had dropped and the streets were hot and quiet, the pavements shadowless under the high sun. Once he saw a dark shape move and his heart leapt, but it was only a cat slinking away behind a fence.

What had Locke been going to do with the stone that first afternoon? Use it to threaten Bur's father – or worse? And Matt's cut had taken ages to heal. When Matt had stolen the stone the previous night, what would it have made him do to Uncle Hodder if he, Edward, hadn't stopped him?

He shuddered, suddenly repelled by the smooth weight of the stone in his hand. He longed to drop it at once. But, as Mae said, he had to find the right place to throw it away – where it would never be found again.

At last, down a narrow side street that ended in a high wall, he saw what he was looking for. It was a derelict cottage; its windows boarded up, the paint on the front door cracked and peeling; and it stood behind a broken fence in an overgrown garden where hollyhocks and wild purple geranium grew rampant. A stunted apple tree stood forlornly in a tangle of bushes at the far end. There was a battered FOR SALE sign leaning at an angle against the fence, and it looked as if it had been there a very long time.

Edward looked around, his heart beating rapidly. He could hear children shouting on the other side of the wall, but a long way off. It must border a recreation ground. There was no one in the street to see what he was going to do.

He drew back his arm. It was then not so much that he threw the stone, but that it seemed to fly from his fingers with tremendous force, piercing the air and shining like jade in the sunlight as it went. Startled, he watched it carve a perfect arc and plummet down towards the apple tree. His fingers tingled as if he had had an electric shock.

Once he had turned the corner and left the cottage behind, he began to feel better. Then, down two neat little streets full of tidy pink and white cottages basking demurely in the sun, he began to have doubts. What if that cottage were sold eventually to a family with kids and one of them found the stone and cut himself as badly as Matt had done? What if the stone brought bad things to the family?

Wearily, he retraced his steps to the cottage. His stomach was grumbling, and the egg and bacon rolls seemed a long time ago. Squeezing through a gap in the broken fence, he found himself in grass so long it brushed his fingertips with a cool dampness. He waded through the web of shade the hollyhocks cast across the grass and squatted down in the undergrowth beneath the apple tree.

But there was no sign of the stone.

He stared up into the tree to see if the stone had caught in a fork, but there was nothing lying between the branches. The stone must have dug itself into the ground with the force of its fall.

Some sort of plant had wound itself around the smooth, knobbly bark of the apple tree, a plant with long green leaves and small, gleaming berries, white as candle wax in the shade. But the stone hadn't caught amongst its tendrils.

The back of Edward's neck prickled in the thick silence. There was something creepy about this place. He'd done his best to find the stone, and now he was getting out of here. If he couldn't find it, surely no one else would?

When Edward arrived back at Gull Cottage longing for his lunch, he found Matt and his uncle on their way out.

'We're going sailing,' Matt said in an offhand way.

Uncle Hodder gave Edward a shy smile of pleasure. 'Matt gave me a call at the shop, and I suddenly thought, "Why not?" It's a wonderful day.'

'But—' said Edward. Fen shook her head at him surreptitiously, and he stopped. *But you're like me*, he thought. *You don't even like sailing that much*.

'Hey, Ed.' Matt tossed him something, which Edward caught automatically. 'My old sunglasses. You can have them. Vali's been shopping in Ipswich with Helga and they bought me a new pair.'

'Cool.' He'd already spotted the very black and shiny pair of sunglasses slung round Matt's neck on a red silk cord. 'Who's Helga? Is she rich?'

'She's Wolf's sister.'

'But Wolf—' He bit his lip, remembering last night: Matt outside the Cross Keys, slurring his words.

'Stop gossiping,' said Fen, 'or you'll never get out on the river, Matt!'

Afterwards, she said to Edward as he munched his way through left-over pizza and salad, 'Hodder's thrilled to be asked to do something with Matt. There was no way he was going to refuse, even if it meant going sailing. It'll do him good to face *Freya*. He's got to come to terms with what happened, and get on with life.'

Edward grunted. He had an uncomfortable feeling that this speech was being directed at him. He'd check out the fishing boats this afternoon, he thought. And he'd go swimming by himself.

He went out on the beach as planned, and began to stroll self-consciously among the fishing boats pulled up on the shingle. Many of them had numbers, rather than names.

He glanced over at the black-tarred wooden shacks and the groups of fishermen greeting each other outside. They had their notices up – FISH, FRESH TODAY, FRESHLY COOKED LOBSTER, CRAB – but no one was buying. The elderly people sitting in the beach shelter watched him without curiosity; otherwise, the shingle was littered with sunbathers reading or lying with their eyes shut against the late afternoon sun.

'Are you going swimming?'

They stood there, the three of them: Lyddie, who had asked the question, Daniel, looking uncomfortable, and another boy who had smooth black hair and thin lips that seemed to curl in contempt at the sight of Edward.

'Maybe.' He made it sound as if he wasn't bothered, one way or the other. He was glad he had Matt's dark glasses on. He didn't need to meet Daniel's eyes.

'You can come with us if you like. He can, can't he, Daniel?'

Daniel nodded and gave Edward a half-smile.

The boy who must be Patrick threw his towel down on the shingle. They were all wearing swimming things. 'I'm going in now. It's far too hot to stand around talking.'

They watched as he ran over the shingle in his beach shoes, and waded into the glittering water. A gentle wave rolled slowly over the surface of the sea and splashed against his chest. He seemed to be stuck where he was, not moving forwards or ducking down into the foam.

'What's the matter?' called Lyddie.

'It's bloody freezing, that's what!' he shouted back. He came out of the water, back across to them, and there were goosebumps over his even tan. 'I'm not swimming in that!'

Daniel looked downcast. 'You can't expect the North Sea to be as warm as where you go on holiday.'

Patrick sat down sullenly and huddled into his towel. Lyddie giggled. 'It's too hot to stand round talking,' she mimicked. 'Come on, both of you!'

Daniel hesitated, looking as if he was torn between staying with his new friend, who hadn't turned out as cool in every situation as he'd thought, and swimming with Edward and Lyddie. Old loyalties won.

They fooled around for a while, splashing and trying to duck each other. In the water it was somehow possible for Edward and Daniel to be as they had always been at Uffenham. You couldn't feel awkward or embarrassed with waves slapping you softly in the face and water bunging up your nose. Patrick's morose figure, swathed in the towel, watched them from the shore.

The sea was cold but seemed to fizz against Edward's skin. He felt it move and lift beneath him, as if he were lying on the smooth pelt of some great, gentle creature as it lolloped along. As it breathed in, it raised him up, so that it seemed he would be drawn into the sky; then, exhaling, it lowered him into deep softness.

The sea was majestic, he thought, primeval – that

was the right word. It had always been there. It brought death but it gave life as well; life had been born out of water. He lay, with Lyddie's happy screams muffled by endless water, and felt something that had been hard and cold and fierce inside him begin to change.

'Hey!' Lyddie bobbed up beside him, sleek as a seal. 'Have you found the boat yet?'

He blew bubbles. 'No.'

'You're not doing it properly, you know.'

Edward roused himself indignantly, standing in the water. 'I can't search all the time!' He lowered his voice and glanced at Daniel, who was wading towards the beach. 'Anyway, keep quiet about it, do you understand? No one's to know.'

Lyddie looked indignant in turn. 'I can keep a secret! I'm not stupid. Anyway, what I meant was that you should look for it in an organized way. You should set yourself a timetable, take all the different areas in Uffenham in turn. There are boats down in the caravan park, you know, and in some of the gardens and garages. They're all over the place.'

'I don't need telling!'

'So you still don't want any help?'

She was trying not to look as if his answer mattered. Her huge eyes, ringed by spiky, wet eyelashes, met his.

Suddenly he found himself smiling.

CHAPTER ELEVEN

The Sea God

Even with Lyddie's help, a week went by without finding *Ringhorn*, and Edward grew desperate.

During that time things were changing at Gull Cottage, but in his misery and frustration he was hardly aware of them. He did notice, however, that his uncle no longer looked so grey and drawn. During the afternoon's sail with Matt he had caught the sun, and he had begun to leave his dark glasses off when he went to work.

At breakfast on Friday, the day before the Carnival, they were both down in the kitchen early. His uncle was taking the day off to help Fen with the preparations.

In a companionable, conspiratorial way, they sliced bread for toast and took the milk and butter out of the fridge, cocooned by the quietness of the cottage. When they sat down at the table together, Edward encouraged his uncle to talk about some of the old and valuable books in his shop. He was surprised at how enthusiastic and interesting he was; he seemed relaxed and pleased to be talking alone with Edward, and Edward relaxed with him.

It was a double shock, almost a betrayal, when after a short pause his uncle remarked in a quite different voice, low and hesitant, 'I know what you must think about me, Edward. I've been wanting to say this for a long time but – well, haven't had the courage, I suppose.'

Edward went on eating his cornflakes, but they might have been scraps of cardboard in his mouth. His heart began to beat in a familiar, sick-making rhythm, like it always did when he suspected someone was going to talk about Dad.

Uncle Hodder pushed a blob of marmalade to one side of his place and looked at his smeared knife blankly. 'I feel so guilty.'

'*Guilty*?' said Edward, startled.

'You must blame me for not going with your father that day.'

'No – of course I don't.'

'You know . . .' His uncle stared out of the window, where a seagull wheeled, startlingly white against an overcast sky, a chip in an iron-grey saucer. 'You know, I've tried to hide the reason from myself all this time. It was because I was scared, Edward. I'm scared of the sea, always have been, and that day the clouds were building up – white horses on the water.'

Edward tried to speak, but his uncle held up a hand. 'I tried to stop him. I said, "Don't go, Bill, it's crazy on your own." But he'd only come up for the weekend, and nothing would stop him. He said, he said—' To Edward's dismay, his uncle's face crumpled, then he got it under control.

'He laughed. "It's a challenge, Hodder," he said. "You're such a coward." And then he went off.' His uncle's dark eyes looked sadly at Edward. 'He was right, wasn't he?'

Edward took a deep breath. 'It wasn't your fault. You couldn't have done anything.'

It was the best he could manage, but it was enough. His uncle's face lightened imperceptibly. He reached out a hand, as if to touch him, but something in Edward's face made him rest it palm upwards on the table between them instead.

'I used to sail with your father because he asked me.' He smiled crookedly. 'Now I'm doing it with Matt for the same reason.'

Edward hesitated. All sorts of words rushed through his head but the ones that came out now were not the right ones. He was spoiling his secret, but he couldn't help it.

'One day you could sail with Dad again.'

132

There was a sudden silence. His uncle looked confused.

Edward leaned over the kitchen table, trying to explain. 'You see, there's an island—'

His uncle cleared his throat, uncomfortably. 'There's an island for us all, Ed, in the end.'

'Yes, that's what I mean,' said Edward eagerly. 'Dad's on an island!'

'You must believe what you feel is right,' said his uncle apologetically. 'I don't know what they teach you in schools these days.'

'No,' said Edward, feeling uncomfortable himself now. 'No, it's nothing to do with that.'

He suspected his uncle was as relieved as he was, when a moment later Fen swept into the kitchen in her Chinese dressing-gown and prevented further explanations. She rubbed the sleep from her eyes, then she and the embroidered dragon on her back glared at them. 'I think the least I might expect, after three paintings delivered to that horrid little shop, let alone the float to organize today, is a cup of tea in bed!'

Edward and his uncle leapt as one man, and with such alacrity, to switch on the kettle, that they almost cannoned into each other.

'Why do you keep staring at the sea?' Lyddie asked Edward that afternoon, as they were trudging back along the coast road after checking the marshy fields between Uffenham and Thorpeness to no avail.

'There's an island out there,' he muttered, gazing at the horizon, where mist hung like a veil of dark-blue chiffon. 'Some days I can see it and some days I can't.'

'I've never seen it.'

'It's going further away, that's why. It hasn't been there for days. It's because we're not getting anywhere with this search. That's why Locke hasn't been bothering to follow us either.'

She looked at him in alarm. 'You're weird.'

'You don't understand!' He made an effort to keep his voice calm. 'Dad's on the island! I've got to get there!'

There was a silence. Lyddie, frowning, looked over at the shingle beyond the road, and at the dark, gently rolling waves beyond the shingle. At last she said wanly, 'We'll never find this boat. I'm not looking for it any more.'

'Fine. I never asked you to help me. You asked yourself because you were bored!'

'That's not true!'

Then, out of nowhere, it seemed, a black Mini overtook them, speeding in the direction of Uffenham. It stopped with a screech of brakes.

'Ed-waard! Ed-waard!'

Vali's blonde head was hanging out of the

passenger window. The driver was the girl he had once seen on the beach with Vali and Matt, a pale girl with long, dark hair, and there was someone else, a boy, sitting in the back.

'Come on, quick!' said Lyddie. 'Perhaps they'll offer us a lift!'

'There's no room,' said Edward, but Lyddie, who had met Vali before, had begun to run.

'You like a lift, Edward?' said Vali, as they came up. 'And your girlfriend?' She winked at Lyddie.

'Thanks,' he muttered, covered in confusion.

Vali got out and pulled her seat forward so they could climb into the back, next to the boy. She was wearing jeans but the other girl was wearing jodhpurs and there were two hard hats up on the shelf behind the back seat.

'That is Nick, next to you. This is my friend, Helga,' said Vali, beaming. 'She is Wolf's sister, and Nick's also. We have been horse-riding together.'

The girl turned and stared at Edward, as he climbed in and sat down awkwardly next to the boy. He noticed with a shock that her eyes were so dark they didn't seem to have pupils; they were like two black holes in her head. 'Er – riding. That's nice,' he said feebly.

'I see you have new sunglasses, Edward,' said Vali, flashing him a teasing smile. 'I think I shout at the wrong boy! They suit you so very much.'

Edward took off his sunglasses sheepishly. He knew she knew they'd been Matt's. He caught the boy looking at him, narrow eyes in a pasty face. The feel of the boy's long, thin legs pressed against his sent a chill of revulsion through him as Helga started the car with a roar.

''S Nick,' said the boy, nodding. 'Helga's my ssister.' His mouth dangled loosely.

'Snick, we call him,' said Helga, and she grinned at Edward in the mirror. He felt very uncomfortable.

'Could you drop me at North Path?' said Lyddie.

'And for you, Edward?' said Vali. 'Gull Cottage? They all prepare for the Carnival there. I come to help later.'

'Um, no, not Gull Cottage,' said Edward guiltily. First he'd try to ask the Newnes sisters about *Ringhorn* again. 'At the top of the High Street, if you can stop.'

Helga's coal-black eyes looked at him in the driving mirror without expression, and then she suddenly spoke in a husky drawl. 'Having fun were you, just now?'

He managed to mutter something non-committal, but he was thankful when they reached Uffenham and he could climb out of the car. He hadn't liked the way Helga's black, enigmatic eyes had met his and seemed to know all about him. As the car drove off he could see her still watching him in the driving mirror.

Mae was on her own, in the dim back room of the cottage in Neptune Alley, a tea tray on the table beside her. She looked delighted to see him. 'I've been so bored, dear, waiting on my own for you. You haven't been to see me for ages.' She gave a little pout.

'I've been busy searching,' he said indignantly.

'You're here now anyway, at just the right time. Zelma's upstairs sitting with *him* – she likes to be with him on her own – and Astrid's out at the supermarket. I told her it was my turn, but she wouldn't listen, bossy old cat.'

She sat him down in Zelma's armchair and plied him with cups of thin, lemony tea and her favourite sugar biscuits. 'Did you get rid of it?' she said, between genteel sips of the tea.

'What? Oh, the stone.' Edward nodded.

'Never, never tell.'

He said quickly, before she went daft on him, 'Is there any change in Bur?' He pushed his hands into his jeans pocket and touched the message, now crumpled to a paper ball.

She sucked in her cheeks. 'I'm afraid not, dear, seeing that *Ringhorn*'s not found yet.'

'It's impossible when I don't know anything about her!' Zelma was the one he needed to question, but Mae would have to do. He put down his teacup and prowled round the little room restlessly, as if it might yield up a vital clue. 'Where were you born, Mae?'

'In a land of ice and snow, dear.'

'The same place as Bur?'

'That's right. More tea, dear?'

It was like talking to a small child, he thought, exasperated. He wasn't going to get anywhere. He stared at the mantelpiece. 'Did those things come from there?'

'Some of them, some we were given.' She pointed at the eye and gave a cackle of glee. 'He tried to steal our knowledge, you know. Much good did it do him!'

The eye seemed to be staring at him in a disagreeable way and he moved on hastily. He could see she had nearly finished the jigsaw. Now he looked more closely at the picture he noticed an odd thing. The huge tree was in full leaf, but the artist had drawn bricks instead of bark over the trunk. A red squirrel peered from a hole in the brickwork, and through the top-most leaves he saw the fierce head of an eagle.

'It's missing two pieces,' said Mae.

'Perhaps they've dropped on the floor. Shall I look?'

'No point, dearie. They'll be found in time.'

He shrugged. 'What are you going to do now you've finished it?' He looked round. 'It's so dark in here. You should get out into the sunshine.'

'My old eyes, dear. The light hurts them.'

Edward slid his sunglasses on to the table beside her. 'If you wore these, you could go out in bright sunlight whenever you wanted. You could watch the Carnival tomorrow and see your costumes!' He watched carefully for her reaction. Perhaps, like a small child, she might be tempted by them.

She stroked the mock-tortoiseshell frames, and a small flicker of greed crossed her face. 'They're very pretty, dear. Could I perhaps – borrow them?'

'You can have them if you tell me something.'

She knew what he meant at once. 'But I can't remember anything about *Ringhorn*, dear. I told you.'

'You must remember something. Try them on, if you like.'

He felt ashamed as soon as she put the sunglasses on. Her old, puckered mouth smiled under the big, dark frames; she looked delighted with herself, like a little girl dressing up. He hardened his heart.

'You can keep them if you help me.'

She whispered it, so that he had to bend to hear. 'Don't ask me, ask the sea god. He knows all secrets to do with the sea. He'll know where she's hidden.'

'The sea god? What do you mean?'

She shook her head.

'That's not fair! You've got to tell me what you mean!'

He tried to snatch the glasses back, but to his horror he couldn't take them from her face; it was as if they were stuck to the bridge of her nose with glue. She giggled crazily. 'They're mine now!'

And however much Edward cajoled her, she wouldn't say a word more.

At Gull Cottage the small sitting-room was filled with costumes and strangers and loud voices. Fen could be heard issuing instructions from the kitchen, Uncle Hodder was dodging about offering mugs of tea and Matt was standing in the middle of it all looking helpless. His expression brightened when he saw Edward.

'Your turn now! I've had my fitting. I'm off to see Vali.'

'Hey, don't leave me,' Edward said in alarm. 'Vali's coming here to help, anyway. She said.'

'Well, maybe I can meet her halfway and put her off. Looks like Fen's got all the help she needs.' Matt gave a sly grin. 'You're going to love your costume!'

'Why?' said Edward suspiciously.

'It's a cracker. You're a mini sea deity, complete with harp!'

'Edward!' Fen's voice was closer. Matt winked. 'I'm off, and you never saw me go!'

'Edward? At last!' Fen emerged, looking flushed and exasperated, her bright eyes snapping. 'Load of fools, this year's helpers!' she hissed into his ear. 'Can't get anything done. If only Hodder would stop doling out tea!' In an ordinary voice she said, 'Can you do something for me? Matt can give you a hand. Be a love, and fetch the sea god?'

Edward started. 'The sea god?'

'Oh, blooming heavens, don't say you've caught the bug, too! In the Marine Street garage, child, the figure that's taking pride of place in the float!'

'Oh, that sea god!'

Fen spread her hands. 'Is there another?'

He went out obediently, taking the garage key with him, glad to get away. There was no sign of Matt, of course, but the figure was light enough to manage on his own.

Daylight from the street streamed into the garage as he pushed the door up over his head, and he saw that the bags and boxes he had put in there had already been taken. The sea god was still propped up in the corner, but it now towered incongruously over a parked car.

He went over to the figure, then hesitated. He looked up at the blank eye-holes. Close to, he could see where the tinfoil had been glued on in curved fish scale shapes and where the newspaper mâché hadn't been painted evenly.

He cleared his throat. 'Where's *Ringhorn*?' he whispered, feeling more stupid than he'd ever felt.

The faint sound of traffic in the High Street, mixed with the mewling of seagulls, came drifting into the garage. That was all. What else had he expected?

Though the figure was light, its height made it awkward to carry. As he staggered outside, a blustery wind was coming off the sea, blowing down the alleyways from the Parade. It caught at the silvery limbs, and he had to pin them down with his arms to the amusement of passers-by. Then the foil armour began to puff out with air so that he was afraid it might come unstuck. It was a relief to reach Gull Cottage and dump the figure in the garden.

Uncle Hodder helped him secure it to the fence with twine, and found some sacking to put over it. 'Should be OK out here,' he said. 'There's no rain forecast tonight.'

Indoors was back to normal; everyone had disappeared home with their costumes and Fen was looking much more cheerful. 'The garments those old ladies made are extraordinary,' she said to Edward. 'The odd thing is, I couldn't take everyone's measurements at the time, but they've needed no alterations at all!'

Matt was still out with Vali, and the three of them had fish and chips from the High Street. Outside twilight fell, and the rising wind rattled the windows.

Fen looked out as she drew the curtains. 'I think we'll have to fit the sea god inside somehow. It would be awful if it blew away.'

'I'll get it,' said Edward, and fetched his penknife from upstairs to cut the twine.

The little garden lay in shadow, but he could see that the sacking had already fallen off the figure. It stirred and shifted in the wind, looking eerily as if it was waking from sleep.

He cut it free, ready to carry it in, but at that moment a strong gust blew, cold and sea-smelling, stinging his bare forearms. It billowed under the silver foil, making the figure's torso ripple with muscles of air. He tried to hold it down as he had before, but he was suddenly fighting the growing strength of the wind, and now it was blowing the figure away from him, against the garden gate.

'Fen!' he shouted. 'Uncle Hodder!' But the kitchen window was shut now and the curtains were drawn so they couldn't see him. Then the wind blew the gate open and the figure was sailing through and down the alleyway at the back of the cottage, still somehow upright. Its helmet flashed in the light from a lamppost in Marine Street.

Edward flung himself through the gate, making a dive for the figure. But Marine Street was a windtrap. He was pushed along himself, and all the while the silver figure was a little way ahead, casting a long black shadow behind it.

This is unreal! he thought, in panic. He had to get it back before the tinfoil was torn to ribbons by the wind. Then he realized he would be lucky to get it back at all, it was being blown along so fast; uncannily upright still, but several inches above the pavement. With the wind beneath him, Edward felt as if he were sailing too. The tips of his trainers hardly touched the ground. He'd never run so fast.

Finally, when they were almost past the last houses, just before the dirt road that led to the river and the sailing club, he caught up with it.

'Got you!'

But in his grasp the figure twisted and pulled in the wind as if it were alive. The tinfoil armour felt ice-cold. One silver arm came up with a new weight and strength, almost knocking him over, outflung in the direction of the marshes. There was a tearing sound, and the torso tugged away from his frantic hands once more, towards the darkness of the dyke path.

CHAPTER TWELVE

Night Mare

Beyond the town, the sky was immense and pale as an opal, sucking all the light out of the land beneath, so that the marshes lay in windswept, reedy darkness. Edward was on the top of the dyke now, with the black river stretching away below on one side and the dyke ditch on the other. Rushing air buffeted him. It was hard to breathe, harder still to stand upright.

'I'll get you!' he grunted, through gritted teeth. The float would look nothing without its centrepiece.

But it was blown on, always just out of his reach, a dark, grotesque shape, swaying stiffly from side to side as the wind held and pulled it.

He was alone in the growing dusk. Fear filled him suddenly, as if the cold wind had pierced the nooks and crannies of his body, filled him with air, like the figure. He imagined both of them blown endlessly onwards until he missed his footing and fell, and was sucked like paper himself into the black mud of the river. Why he didn't turn back he didn't know; a wild determination drove him on.

Then, all at once, it was over. The wind dropped. The great figure, unsupported, tottered and collapsed. It dived like a kite full-length on the path against a clump of tall grasses, one arm towards the river.

Edward staggered up to it. His heart was pounding from the chase, but it had been worth it. The figure was still in one piece and they should be able to repair it.

The outflung arm was hard to disentangle from the coarse, damp grass of the bank. He scrambled down the side of the dyke to free it. There was the ruined hull of a small boat lying half-buried in the mud below him. He'd seen this little creek in daylight. He'd sketched here with Fen before the search for *Ringhorn* began.

Though the wind had dropped, there was a thrumming in his ears. It grew steadily louder. Hooves, coming towards him along the ridge of the dyke. Now he could see the black silhouette of a rider on a horse against the luminous sky. The rider was a young woman, long dark hair streaming out behind her, and her horse was a great black brute, snorting and blowing out wreaths of steaming breath.

Edward edged away down the slope. He wasn't

afraid of horses, but this one looked as if it would trample down everything in its way. Then he realized that the sea god lay directly in its path.

'Stop! Please! Let me—' His voice seemed tiny in all that space, drummed into nothing by the hooves. He caught a glimpse of the girl's exultant face, a flash of teeth.

It was Helga. She was laughing, and her laughter was wild. She reined in her horse and it rose above him, its powerful front legs raking the empty air. He thought she was letting him reach the figure.

'Thanks,' he gasped, crawling up the slope.

To his amazement, as he lunged forward to rescue the paper figure, the girl let the horse forward deliberately. Its great hooves trampled the silver fish scales; they crushed the figure into the earth and grass so that the wire framework bent and buckled and papier-mâché bulged from the limbs.

Edward felt an enormous fury surge through him. A voice in his head seemed to say quite clearly down the years, 'It's the Night Mare. But you can hold the reins.'

Without thinking, he shot out his right hand to grasp the reins. It came up against a tremendous heat, solid, like a wall. Through it he could see a shuddering darkness that blotted out the sky. For a second he touched something smooth that might have been leather or horseflesh.

There was a searing pain in his hand. He thought he smelled his own flesh scorching, and in horror he leapt back, into nothing. There was no ground beneath him, only air. Then he hit the slope of the dyke and began sliding down, unable to get a foothold on the dewy grass.

There was mud at the bottom. His hip and his left leg and foot sank in deeply; it seemed wonderfully cool and soft. He lay there, winded, gasping for breath, his head against the slope and his cheek resting on hairy strands of grass. His hand was all burning pain, to the bone.

But when at last he raised his head, the horse and its rider had gone, dissolved into the dusk as if they were formed from darkness themselves.

Pieces of the sea god were scattered everywhere, stuck into the damp earth of the path. Only one limb was whole, the same arm that had been trapped in the bank, the arm that seemed to point down at the shell of the little boat.

Edward's heart gave a strange flutter. He staggered to his feet, mud oozing round his ankles. Out of the wind in the lee of the dyke, he could hear the plash and ripple of water spilling in with the rising tide, slapping against the timbers of the boat. He had to hurry.

At each step his trainers filled with mud; it sucked

at his feet as he tried to pull them free. But at last his fingers touched damp wood.

What a fool he was! This boat must have lain here for years! And it was too dark to see a name, even if it hadn't been worn away by weather. In despair he clutched at the side of the boat to steady himself in the rising water.

And then he felt it. A raised pattern on the wood. Three circles, overlapping.

'Edward.'

There was a ghostly white figure standing beneath the dyke ridge, only a few metres away. He jumped in shock before he saw that it was Mae, bundled into a pale mackintosh, her white hair blown back, her little body propped on a stick like a magician's wand.

He was too astonished to speak. He'd never have thought she could walk so far. And how had she known he was here?

'Well done, dear. You've found her. You see, Zelma knew you'd succeed.' Her voice sounded stronger than usual.

'But I don't understand. How can this boat be *Ringhorn*?'

'Locke has disguised her. This shape hides another. But he couldn't disguise her name. Look.'

She took something from her pocket and a beam of light fell on the little boat. The rotting hull showed clearly. Edward's eyes hurt with the dazzle, and then he saw letters on the stern, not painted but carved into the wood. *Ringhorn*.

'But why didn't you tell me Locke might change her?' he cried out.

'How could I, child?' She was calm. 'You'd have given up.'

'I wouldn't!' *Never, not for Dad's sake*. Confused emotions battled inside him: anger and hurt at her lack of trust, overwhelming relief. 'So I can go to the island?'

'None of her parts must be missing.' There was something strange in Mae's voice, a warning?

He stared into the beam of light. He couldn't see the old woman beyond it. He began to tremble with anxiety and cold and his burnt hand felt on fire. 'I thought you said this was a disguise?'

'She'll be made whole in the changing, but even so, none of her parts must be missing.' The light played over the hull, as if she meant him to look.

'The rudder's there, though it's split,' he said falteringly. 'But I can't see any tiller.'

'I knew it couldn't be so easy, I knew he'd play his tricks, the Sly One. What use is she without a tiller?'

'But where is it?'

'He'll have destroyed it. He wants to sap Bur of his soul's strength by trapping him here.'

'What can we do, then?'

'Come out of that mud, you poor child. Come close. Words carry on the wind.'

Somehow he waded back through water that had almost reached his knees, shielding his eyes against the light. He felt heavy with disappointment; his wet jeans and T-shirt only added to his misery.

Mae held out an arm. It was surprisingly strong as it clutched him and drew him up the dyke. Halfway up, while they were still sheltered from the wind, she paused to catch her breath and took his other arm. She pressed his burnt hand gently against her own palm, and slowly a blessed coolness took away the heat and hurt. When she spoke her voice was gentle too.

'You did a brave thing, dearie, when you faced that hell horse. Not many dare do that. You've overcome two of his creatures, but he's not called Trickster for nothing. You have the greatest danger to face before *Ringhorn* is made whole again.'

'I can get a new tiller made at the boat yard,' he said, hardly listening in his misery, 'but it'll take days, and I don't know how big it should be.'

'No matter. Like *Ringhorn* herself, the tiller must be made from the great ash tree. It will know its own. Measurements don't matter in the old magic ways.'

'You mean the tiller has to be made from ash?'

'There is only one tree like that. It holds all our lives. Now come. We mustn't linger.'

The wind, driving over the marshes, hit them full in the face as they reached the top of the dyke, and took away his questions. But Edward was too despairing to care. He bent and picked up the one silver arm that was all that was left of the sea god.

Mae tottered on her stick and took his resisting arm. 'I'm too old for this sort of thing.' But his side was stiff against her as he clutched the silver limb, and he couldn't speak.

They followed her beam of light all the way along the dyke path to the grit road, though Edward couldn't be sure it was a torch she held. He had the strangest feeling that she wasn't there at all, that he was supporting nothing but a bundle of clothes, she was so little and light. But she made it to the end, and her voice, old, tired and relieved, quavered in his ear, 'There's my taxi.'

She had turned her light out and all Edward could see was the dark shape of some waiting vehicle. She left his side surprisingly quickly and her words floated back to him. 'The ash tree! Don't delay. Then the bargain can be kept.'

'Mae! Wait!' he shouted desperately. 'You've got to help me!'

Though no sound of an engine came to him, nor could he see any headlights, the dark shape began to move rapidly away. Suddenly he was alone, and freezing cold, his wet clothes pressed against him by the wind. She hadn't even offered him a lift, he thought bitterly.

He didn't know how he made it down the grit road in the darkness, shivering so violently he could hardly walk.

There were two figures emerging from the lighted beginning of the High Street. One of them began to run towards him, followed by the other.

Fen reached him before Matt. 'Edward! I couldn't think what had happened to you! Hodder's searching the other way.'

He thrust the broken limb of the sea god at her, but he couldn't say anything at all.

CHAPTER THIRTEEN

Where All Times Meet

'It doesn't matter, Ed,' said Fen.

They were back together in the sitting-room of Gull Cottage. Edward had changed into dry clothes, and they were drinking hot chocolate: Matt and he sprawled on the carpet, Fen and his uncle in armchairs. 'It's a shame about the figure, but it doesn't matter because—' She disappeared for a moment and came back with something that glittered in her arms. 'Because *this* costume was left over. It's one of the ones made by the Newnes sisters. I never asked them to make it, but here it is!'

'Sea god's armour!' breathed Edward. He stared at silver fish scales that seemed to ripple and move, sparkling with brilliant rainbow colours as they caught the light. This armour had a living sheen. It couldn't be made from tinfoil!

'And a cloak! And a helmet!' she said, flourishing them triumphantly.

The cloak was sea-coloured, changing from palest azure to darkest storm-green, and it flowed like a wave from her hand. A layer of fishermen's net lay over it, in which small shells and tiny dried fish gleamed like pearls. The helmet was so studded with shells and stones it looked like the fossilized head of some great sea-creature.

Some enchantment held them all as the shining costume swayed in the light. Uncle Hodder rubbed his eyes. His face was confused, as if he was dreaming. 'Remarkable! Look at the workmanship!'

Had the Newnes sisters known all along what was going to happen tonight? thought Edward. 'Who's going to wear it?' he asked.

Matt raised a hand ruefully.

'He was the only one it fitted,' said Fen. 'He's tall enough to carry the armour, and he's filled out a bit these holidays.'

'Must be your cooking, Fen.' Matt's grin was wide.

'He's always had a big head, of course,' said Edward. He rolled away from Matt's kick and looked down at his hand resting on the carpet. He'd forgotten how much the burn had hurt. Now when he uncurled the palm he saw it was unmarked. The whole incident with the horse might have been a dream. But he'd found *Ringhorn*!

He staggered suddenly to his feet and the room swayed round him in a surprising way. 'I must go and see the Newneses.'

'Not now?' exclaimed Fen.

'I've got to.'

'I'm sorry, Edward, but you can't go visiting at this hour,' said Fen flatly. 'Poor old ladies, they'll be tucked up in bed! And you're dropping! Do you realize what time it is?'

'Quarter to midnight,' said Uncle Hodder, waking from a doze and rousing himself from his armchair with a groan. 'And the float arrives in the car park at eight tomorrow. We've got to get all the stuff down there and have it decorated by eleven for the Parade. Why do we do this every year?'

'Haven't a clue,' said Matt cheerfully. 'Come on, little brother!' and he gave Edward an unbrotherly push out of the room. 'There's time for a few hours' kip before you try your costume on tomorrow morning!'

Edward dragged himself up the stairs reluctantly, but there was never any point in arguing with Fen. He'd have to slip off sometime in the morning while the float was being decorated. Secretly, he was relieved not to go out again tonight; he felt exhausted.

The moon was shining into their room. Dark rags of cloud blew across its face, and beneath it the patch of sea that showed between the rooftops was black as ink. He stared out, the wind cold on his face. Was it his imagination, or was the horizon not entirely flat? Was his island there again?

Matt threw his clothes off with his usual speed, and bounded beneath his duvet. 'Do you mind being the sea god?' Edward asked him, leaving the window open a crack.

''Course not. Funky costume. It'll be a laugh.'

Edward looked at Matt sitting up in bed, his fair hair tousled, half-smiling at him. 'You've changed, you know that?'

'It's Hodder that's changed, not me. The old stick's been quite chatty ever since we went sailing. He's going to organize a summer job for me next year at Uffling Hoo. We're going to the site on Monday.'

'But I thought you'd had it with archaeology?'

Matt stopped smiling, but he didn't snap Edward's head off as he was expecting. He lay back with his long arms crossed behind his head and spoke quietly, looking up at the low ceiling, not at Edward. 'I've decided there'll be some things I'll do for Dad – sort of in his memory – and some things I'll do for me. I'm not sure what archaeology is yet, that's why I've got to give it another go. If it's going to be for life, then it's got to be for me. It's my life, after all.'

He lay down and shut his eyes. 'Get that light off before I clobber you, Ed!'

By morning the wind had dropped completely and the sun was sparking and bouncing off the High Street.

Edward's jeans were still damp, so he left them where he'd shoved them last night – in a bundle under his bed – and pulled on his combats without bothering to transfer the message. It would be impossible anyway to slip off to Neptune Alley before the parade of floats was over.

He was right: Fen gave him endless jobs running between Gull Cottage and the car park, and fixing decorations on to the float; then, as soon as he had finished, she insisted he tried his costume on back at the cottage so she could see if it fitted.

'It's your fault, Ed. You weren't around yesterday.'

'I look like a lump of seaweed,' groaned Edward. His was not one of the costumes made by the Newnes sisters.

'What's wrong with seaweed?' retorted Fen, wiping one of his green fronds out of her eyes. She was kneeling below him to pin on a frond that had come loose. 'The Chinese consider it a delicacy.' She paused, then added suddenly, 'You know, it's nice of you to go and see those old ladies so much, and they *were* wonderful making those costumes for me . . .' She hesitated. 'But I wonder if they aren't a bit *odd*?' She knelt back on her heels and gave him one of her sharp brown glances. 'You do seem to be getting rather obsessed with them, Ed.'

He made a non-committal noise, but was forced to stay there while she crawled round his knees, checking the hem. 'Or is it something else?' she continued relentlessly. 'There's nothing worrying you, is there? You seem in a world of your own at the moment.'

'There's nothing,' he said flatly. *Only getting to the island.*

'Good.' She stopped crawling, and looked up at him, not altogether as if she believed him.

He hesitated. 'Do you know if there are any ash trees round here?'

'You don't get much ash in Suffolk. Too dry.'

'Do you know this bit of poem, then? "And the bud grows dead on the world ash tree"?'

She was half-laughing now, in mock despair. 'What is all this? Never heard of it. Too long since my O levels. Now go and ask Vali to do your make-up or we'll never be ready!'

He thought he saw Mae several times during the parade, as the farm tractors drove through the crowded streets, drawing the floats on trailers behind them. Once she was standing behind a group of children in fancy dress, once she was by the Lady Mayor's dais. She was wearing the sunglasses. He didn't know if she saw him. She might not have recognized him anyway in the awful costume and green face paint.

'Look!' cried Vali, unrecognizable too in her gold mermaid's wig and coral circlet. 'Look, there's Helga!' She waved madly, her bare arm sparkling with glitter gel, and dislodged one of the papier-mâché rocks with the end of her outsize comb.

'Don't!' hissed Edward, in a mixture of embarrassment and horror. He couldn't bear to catch Helga's knowing eyes. But the rock had fallen off the side of the float and was bouncing towards the crowd.

A young man pushed forward, swarthy, dark-haired, sunlight glinting on a single earring. He picked up the rock with one hand and, with a mocking bow, tossed it back to Vali.

'Thank you, Wolf,' she said demurely, giving him a long, grateful look from beneath green-mascaraed eyelashes. She turned, smiling. 'That was kind, Matt, no?' Matt, imprisoned and powerless on his rocky throne and rendered speechless by his helmet, quivered with emotion.

Edward ignored them both. As Wolf went back into the crowd his gaze followed him. He saw him leap lightly up the steps of the lifeboat shed and join three figures standing on the balcony that ran round it. They were in shadow, but Edward knew them.

Locke, with Helga, Snick and now, Wolf. Locke, with his three sinister children, watching the Carnival. He should have realized long ago that they belonged together. As the float rolled on, he saw them turn their heads simultaneously to watch it pass. Or were they watching him? He wondered bitterly if Locke knew he'd found *Ringhorn*. He must be gloating over his destruction of the tiller, certain that Edward could do nothing more to help Bur.

But he was going to surprise Locke, he thought. He wasn't going to give up.

After the parade, the floats finished up in the car park again, at the end of the town. They would be dismantled after lunch. Vali took off her tail, and everyone on Fen's float began to talk and stretch with relief; some of the costumes were heavy.

Edward touched his stiff green face gingerly. The sun had hardened the make-up to a mask. He tapped Matt's sea god headpiece. 'Anyone at home? You can come out now.'

Matt's hands reached up and took off the helmet. 'Weird.' He put it down carefully on his rocky throne and rubbed his eyes, looking pale in the bright sunlight.

'What is?' said Edward.

Matt hesitated. 'The eye pieces seem to make everything go blurry – like being underwater.'

'Let's have a look.' Edward put out a green hand.

'No!' Matt's hand slammed down over his. 'Sorry,' he said, more calmly. 'It's just that . . . You're weird enough already, Ed!'

Nonplussed, Edward swung his legs over the side of the float. 'Well, I'm off to get this muck off my face and see what's for lunch!'

'Fen will have forgotten about such unimportant things as lunch, you poor kid. She'll have been chasing the float. She'll turn up any minute to give us more orders.'

Edward's mind was on the afternoon. He leapt off and made for the High Street. He'd have something to eat, then go to Neptune Alley.

Crowds jostled him, looking for refreshment stalls. Music jangled from the sea front, where there were dodgems and children's roundabouts by the boating pond. Uffenham was transformed for its day, the cottages along the High Street nestling in a cat's cradle of brightly coloured bunting.

'I saw you taking part earlier,' said a voice in his ear.

Edward swung round. He felt the blood rush to his face under the green paint. At least he wasn't hiding the message anywhere in his costume.

'My family and I were admiring your float during the parade. Most artistic.' Locke smiled at Edward, and his pale blue eyes creased at the corners. 'I don't suppose you've come across that young cousin of mine today, have you? All these people – I was certain we'd bump into each other.'

'No,' said Edward truthfully. They stared at each other. Edward felt scorched by Locke's hot gaze, unable to escape before the next question. He was sure it would be about *Ringhorn*. At last Locke would expose his own actions and would trap Edward into doing the same.

But what Locke said next took him completely off guard. 'I lost something recently, something that I value. A stone.' He laughed. 'Sounds strange, doesn't it, to talk of stones having any worth. But you'd know it if you found it. It's quite different from the shingle of Uffenham. Be careful, it's sharp. Must have cut a hole in my trouser pocket and fallen out.'

The green paint was stiff on Edward's face. He hoped it hid his expression.

'You see,' said Locke. 'The strange thing is I seem to *smell* it hereabouts. It is here, or has been. It doesn't smell of the sea, you see.' His nose seemed to lengthen and point like a fox's muzzle as he looked down the High Street. For an extraordinary second Edward could see the red hairs inside his nostrils tremble, as if indeed he scented some faint, stony bitterness still lingering around Gull Cottage. Then the impression was gone, and the charm was back. 'Are you sure you haven't anything to tell me?'

Edward, his mouth too dry to speak, shook his

head. He was thankful that people were passing them on either side.

Locke looked up, straight into the sun, and then down at Edward again. His red hair seemed to flash with fire. 'A pity. But I think you'll want to tell me something very soon.' A bark of laughter and he was gone, striding off at his usual speed into the crowd.

Edward let himself thankfully into the safety and silence of Gull Cottage. He tore off his costume with shaking hands and got down to scrubbing all the parts of himself that were green. By the time he'd finished much of the paint seemed to have transferred itself to the kitchen sink.

He dried himself on a tea towel, changed back into his combats and T-shirt and made a couple of huge sandwiches. No one else turned up while he was eating. Then he went to fetch the message. Now he'd found *Ringhorn*, surely Bur would have recovered enough to read it at last.

But the jeans weren't under his bed anymore. In fact, the usual pile of clothes he kept conveniently to hand beneath it had vanished altogether, and it didn't take a genius to know what had happened to them. Fen – being domestic.

With a sinking heart Edward leapt down the stairs. The orange plastic laundry basket was empty and so was the washing-machine. Out in the garden amongst a medley of his and Matt's clothes on the washing-line, he found his jeans dangling limp and defeated-looking but undeniably clean. And there was no message in the upside-down pocket. He hunted everywhere – in the grass and back in the kitchen. Fen had retrieved his Swiss Army penknife and put it on a shelf, but that was all he found. He stowed it away in his combats.

Fen always checked their pockets before she washed anything. She would have saved the message for him, too. He'd ask her later, once he'd been to see the Newnes sisters.

After the noisy crowds in Marine Street, Neptune Alley was deserted and seemed to hold a silence of its own. He went through the archway, crossed to the cottage and rang impatiently on the doorbell.

No one came.

In dismay he pushed at the front door. It wasn't locked after all. It opened on to the dim, damp hall and he went straight down to the back room. But to his surprise there was no one there.

He left the room and ran up the stairs, two at a time. The spare room door was closed. He knocked, but there was no sound from inside, so he turned the handle and pushed it open.

The curtains were pulled a little way back. The sun

came through the gap and shone on to Bur's empty bed, on to the rumpled quilt and Fen's towelling robe, neatly folded at the bottom. Dad's canvas shoes had gone.

Frantically, Edward rushed to the head of the stairs. 'Mae!'

There was no answer, only silence. There was no sea-sound; the empty cottage seemed dead. Time was suddenly stilled. *Keep calm*, he thought, steadying himself on the banisters.

Could they have left him a note?

Downstairs, he searched the back room. He switched on the lamp over Mae's table. There was no note lying there, but she had finished the jigsaw. She had found the two missing pieces: now a human face peered eerily out from the branches and foliage.

He gave up searching for a note, and left the little cottage, closing the front door behind him. He was coming out of Neptune Alley, blinking in the sunlight, when he saw Lyddie loitering on the corner.

'Have you been following me?'

'No, I haven't, honestly. What are you doing?'

'Visiting some people who weren't there.' He couldn't decide whether to tell her he'd found the boat at last. She'd never believe his story.

She didn't notice his hesitation. 'Come on!'

'Where?'

'The Martello tower! Have you forgotten? They're

opening it up to the public today. Everyone's going. That's where your friends will be, I expect.'

In a daze, he felt her take his sleeve and pull it. Still, he'd always wanted to get inside the tower, hadn't he? All those summers trying to climb in with Matt, only to find their way blocked by barbed wire or large, unyielding padlocks. He could go back to Neptune Alley afterwards.

The sea wall was thronged with people, some heading for the tower, some returning; hooting cars caused miniature dust-storms as they drove through the crowd. Today a Union Jack fluttered from the gun platform, but the tower looked no less imposing: a dark stump on the horizon that grew steadily taller as Edward and Lyddie drew closer to the shingle ditch that surrounded it. Barbed wire still covered the windows, but the wooden bridge that led from the mound to the first floor across the ditch was open, and people were walking across to the dark doorway on the other side.

A little girl came running up to them. 'Hi, Lyddie! Are you going in, too?'

'See you,' said Edward hastily. He certainly didn't want to explore the tower in the company of two chattering girls who were younger than him. He began to make his way alone through the lumps of rock on the mound, towards the bridge.

It was then that he saw them.

They were sitting in a row – Mae, Zelma and Astrid – with their backs against one of the large white lumps of concrete, close to the bridge but out of the way of passers-by. They seemed to be having a picnic. They had a Thermos, some plastic mugs and a sandwich box, and they were sitting full in the sun, their faces tilted up to it, their eyes half closed, ignoring the steady flow of visitors over the bridge. The sunlight drained them of colour so that they looked grey and white, like ghosts. It was hard to see them against the grey and white rock. Edward might have missed them altogether.

But they didn't miss him.

The three old faces turned towards him, eyes opening blindly against the dazzle.

'Good afternoon, Edward,' said Mae. She wasn't wearing his sunglasses.

'Good afternoon,' he stammered.

He waited a moment, but arms folded, mouths shut primly, they seemed to be waiting for him. After a minute he said helplessly, 'What are you doing here?'

'Having a picnic, what does it look like?' said Astrid, and Mae gaily raised her mug to him as proof.

'But where's Bur?' he said, bewildered.

'Oh, he's better, much better, thanks to you.' Mae nodded brightly. 'He'll be around somewhere, enjoying the fresh air. Now, have a sandwich, dear. Cucumber or tomato?'

'He hasn't the time,' hissed Astrid, glaring at her. 'More to the point,' she said to Edward, 'why are *you* here? Doing something about a new tiller, I hope.'

'That will do, Astrid,' said Zelma, in her gentle, whispery voice. 'You know why I've brought him here.' She looked up at Edward and patted the ground beside her, so that out of politeness he found himself squatting down obediently. Astrid and Mae were still scowling at each other. Mae took a sandwich and chewed it very slowly, her eyes on Astrid.

'Don't mind them,' whispered Zelma. 'The past always resents the present. For the present, time is infinite, you see, and the past can't forgive that.' Her colourless skin stretched over frail bones, like an ancient mask, as she smiled at him. 'You've done well. You've defeated two of the Trickster's creatures.'

'But he's burnt the tiller!'

'I know. But you mustn't be defeated. Indeed . . .' her curiously opaque eyes stared past him at a future only she could see, '. . . I see that you have much to do.'

'I've only come to visit the tower, you know,' said Edward apologetically.

'But this is where all times meet, my child. That's why we three are here. The tower joins past, present and future, earth, sea and sky. Something awaits you in there. You must find out what it is.'

Unreal, thought Edward, but the conversation

seemed as real as the white sunlight, the murmuring sea beyond the wall and the dark figures of the people crossing the bridge in the shadow of the tower.

He felt Zelma's fingers lightly touch his face, tracing its shape, feeling the strands of straight hair that had flopped over his forehead. 'I chose you. I knew you'd find *Ringhorn*. I know you'll find a new tiller. Now go.'

It was a surprisingly firm dismissal from such a frail old lady. Not daring to argue, Edward blundered to his feet, blinking against the glare. Yet he wanted to ask so much. She must know where he could find the ash tree. Even more vital, she must know if his father was on the island.

But that was a question he'd never have the courage to ask anyway.

He took a few steps and then looked back. They had almost merged with the colour of the rock; but he saw Mae raise her mug to him again, as if she was drinking a toast to wish him well.

He turned and walked over the bridge to the tower.

CHAPTER FOURTEEN

Serpent

It was dark inside the tower, and he sensed rather than saw the other people in there. All his senses felt sharpened. When an arm was stretched in front of him stopping him going further, he jumped back nervously.

'Ticket, young man? Half price, are you?' It was a man dressed in a nineteenth-century military uniform of red jacket and breeches.

'I'm sorry, I haven't any money,' said Edward desperately. He felt in his pockets, but there was only his penknife.

'I've got some.' Lyddie was close behind him, the little girl in tow.

The man winked. 'Lucky you've got a rich girlfriend, eh? First and last chance to see inside, too, mebbe. Tower's been bought by the Trust. It's to be done up and rented out as a holiday home.'

'For people to *live* in?' said Lyddie, wrinkling her nose. '*I* wouldn't fancy it!'

But the first floor of the tower at least was in surprisingly good condition. Low voltage electric lights had been rigged up to give the impression of candlelight, although some daylight filtered in through a couple of slit windows. When Edward's eyes adapted, he saw that the space was divided into three chambers. In one of them the local librarian was acting as guide. A group of people were clustered round her.

'Now, as you all probably know, these towers were built during the Napoleonic Wars as a defence against invasion by France.' She was a forceful, enthusiastic woman who reminded Edward of one of his teachers. 'The chambers here were living quarters for one officer and twenty-four men. The officer would have had one of them to himself, the men would have shared another and the last one would have been used as a storeroom.'

'There's nothing in them now,' complained a child. 'No guns.'

'Aren't the walls thick?' marvelled his mother.

The librarian was in her element. Her eyes shone. 'Yes, four metres thick this side overlooking the sea. Do you know it took half a million bricks to build this tower?'

'Where did them soldiers go to the lavvy?' asked the child, unimpressed.

The librarian wasn't fazed. 'Good question. See that trapdoor? There's a ladder under that which leads down to the ground floor. The latrines would have been down there. And that's where they would have stored gunpowder and ammunition. No, I'm afraid you can't go down, little boy.' She grimaced at his mother. 'Public safety and all that. It's been tricky enough getting permission to open this one floor today. No one's allowed up on the gun platform either.'

Lyddie and her friend grew bored. 'We're going back to the Carnival,' said Lyddie to Edward. 'Want to come?'

'I'll hang around here for a bit, I think.'

The three chambers emptied rapidly of visitors. Edward looked round at the bare fireplaces and the ventilation shafts in the walls, and his anticipation drained away.

There was an enclosed flight of stone steps each side of the chamber leading up to the gun platform on the roof. He stood by the nearest one, peering up. It curved sharply away near the bottom of the steps and he could see nothing beyond the curve. A rope had been hung across the steps at that point to prevent the public going further.

The chamber behind him was filling with people again, and the librarian was repeating her talk. Small children ran round and round the circumference of the first floor, touching the walls, chasing each other. Edward watched them and felt dizzy himself. It was airless in the chamber, and it had been a short night. He yawned, and sat down on the bottom step. In a minute he'd leave.

All at once, he snapped awake. The chamber had darkened and chilled. The librarian was continuing to talk, smiling at the red-haired man and the boy who had just come in together and were standing in the doorway, blocking the exit from the chamber.

Edward panicked. Locke and Snick couldn't see him at the moment because of the people standing in front, but for how long? The only way to avoid being seen was by retreating up the steps a little way and hiding behind the curve.

Just as he was about to duck under the rope, he heard Locke's voice across the chamber floor, raised above the noise of the children: 'I'm sorry to interrupt, Madam, but there's a boy on the right tower steps.' He sounded courteous, concerned.

The chamber was silent, suddenly; the librarian's voice said something, uncharacteristically flustered. Edward heard Locke say, 'My son will fetch him back for you.'

Edward glanced round the curve, saw Snick's pale face jut through the crowd below and his dark eyes narrow as he spotted him; leaping to the steps with his long, thin legs, he called out, 'Snick! Snick!' like a grotesque war cry.

Edward didn't hesitate. He was under the rope and round the curve, climbing as fast as he could. His only chance was to get to the top first, come down the other staircase and hope Locke wasn't waiting.

His breath was coming faster as he climbed, but there was no sound of footsteps behind him: it was absolutely silent except for his own soles slapping on stone. Perhaps Snick had turned back and gone up the other staircase. Perhaps he was already lying in wait for him on the roof.

The steps were steeper now, the air surprisingly cold. But a clear, pale daylight shone on the bricks either side of him. He must reach the gun platform in a minute! But even as he thought that, the stairway did another twist and became narrower, and his fingertips, touching the walls to give him balance as he climbed, grew numb. The bricks glistened with a dark bitter sheen that wasn't water.

Ice!

He had no time to take this in before one of his feet slipped and he almost fell. He was bewildered; but still he climbed on, very carefully now, placing his trainers in the middle of each icy step, noticing that his panting breath came out in white clouds of condensation in the freezing air.

What had happened?

The change when it came was so gradual he hardly noticed it at first. The bricks under his fingers no longer held the cold deadness of stone; the icy sheath that had scraped and numbed his fingers seemed to dissolve. He touched a surface that was ridged and almost warm in comparison, and though the air was still cold, it smelt damper and more pungent. A thick, pale grey dusk, like fog, filled the stairwell.

Suddenly, shockingly, there was an unearthly shriek above him and something large and white came beating down the stairs so fast that he had to press himself against the side to avoid being knocked down. He could hear the bird or whatever it was clattering about below him; then the sound was stifled by the familiar heavy silence.

Trembling, Edward rested where he was for a moment. To his alarm he could see long cracks in the strange fibrous texture of the wall. There was even a small hole. He put his eye to it, but couldn't see anything.

He began to climb again, cautiously. A larger hole appeared on the same level as a step. This was unsafe – in a minute he'd turn back.

Now, even the stairs were changing. His trainers no longer slipped; they clung to a smooth surface, the same texture as the walls. And now he knew what it was.

When he came to the next hole, big as a small

doorway, he forced himself to look out. A narrow bridge, grey as ashes, ending in a fork that led to nothing, stretched away from the tower. It was a bough bare of leaves, and its surface was grooved and ridged as if it had been scoured with a knife. Minor branches grew from it, disappearing into cloud. It was impossible to see anything below.

'The great ash tree!' He looked up at the stairs. He might never reach the top. Yet, if the tiller had to be made from the tree – this tree – all he had to do was to break off a branch.

Edward took a deep breath. He bent down, clutched the sides of the hole with both hands and levered himself out on his stomach. One wriggle and he was free of the hole and the relative safety of the tower, and out in the icy air; he was clinging to the bough with his arms and legs. Below him he sensed a vast nothingness, and from it rose a choking, freezing water vapour that filled his mouth and nostrils.

There were other branches growing from the main trunk on either side of him, sticking out of cloud, and soot-black, dead-looking buds, furred with droplets of water, on the twigs that grew from the branches.

And the bud grows dead on the world ash tree.

He began to worm his way along, looking for a branch to break off, something broad and strong that would do for a tiller. He could feel the ridged bark scratch at his combats and was thankful he wasn't wearing shorts. A thick branch sprouted out just before him, not too short and free of twigs, but to get hold of it he had to let go his grip with one hand.

Very slowly he manoeuvred his nearest hand up towards the branch to hold it at the join. He began to twist it, feeling the bough beneath him move slightly but sickeningly as he did so, so that he had to grip even harder with his knees.

It was too difficult. It needed more force to break it off, and he was scared he'd slip. He lay still, gulping mist into his lungs, and could have wept with frustration.

Then he thought of the penknife in one of his pockets, his Swiss Army penknife with its three blades.

With great care he managed to reach it. He clicked out the largest blade and brought the knife towards the branch. Infinitely slowly, so as not to disturb his balance, he began to move it backwards and forwards across the bark. If he could saw halfway through, then he'd be able to break it off.

A tiny, chilling breeze had got up. It was enough to shift the cloud, pushing it away in drifting cushions and exposing a giant network of branches below him, twisting and turning and branching like huge cables. As the last puffs of cloud floated away, he saw ground alarmingly far below: patches of white that must be snow gleamed between the branches in the grey dusk.

He lifted his head to see what lay beyond the tree, and gasped.

Not far away was a wintry shore. The tree's mighty roots stretched away to touch the snow-covered sand, and beyond the sand the sea curled and dipped in dark-blue frozen motion, each white-capped wave carved in ice. Nothing moved except the tiny disturbance of air around the tree. There was no living creature. The landscape was dead, shrouded in eternal winter.

Before his gaze the scene lurched giddily. He was beginning to suffer from vertigo. He dragged his eyes away and forced himself to concentrate on sawing the branch. Perhaps the light was better with the mist gone, because he now saw something he hadn't noticed before. There was a thin dark line across the branch he was cutting. It ran on to the bough he lay on, and across it, under his chest, and there were similar lines on the other branches around him, all running in a different direction from the natural grooves in the bark, like the pattern of a jigsaw. He couldn't make out how deep they went, but the discovery added to his uneasiness.

The penknife had made only a slight cut in the

wood. It would have to do. He reached down and put the penknife back in his pocket and carefully brought his hand back up to twist the branch.

He had just grasped it when the silence seemed to crack apart. A terrible sound tore at his eardrums. Out at sea the crust of ice was breaking. A great floe shot up and splintered down, creating a hole where water churned and boiled in gigantic fountains. Spray hit his face like a shower of icy pebbles. He yelled with pain and almost lost his balance, but still he gripped the branch.

Not far away something was rising from the seething foam. He screamed, as a vast, monstrous, unbelievable head rose from the water and turned slowly, seeking. Narrow eyes saw him, a tongue flickered.

The whole tree was breaking; the black line beneath him was splitting open. The branch he had sawn came away in his hand and the world turned upside-down.

CHAPTER FIFTEEN

A Golden Prow

He was sucked through darkness by some enormous force. He felt himself squeezed so tightly he couldn't even open his eyes. His ribs were crushed, his back hurt; there was something hard and cold beneath him.

Then time stopped and started again. Edward opened his eyes and saw he was sitting on a step behind the curve of the tower staircase. He was huddled against the inner wall, clasping something heavy across his knees. There was no sound of people below him, and the staircase was shadowy as if evening had come already.

'You're safe. Rest a minute.'

The speaker seemed to materialize from nowhere, a young man Edward didn't recognize. He shrank back into the bricks. Then he saw the canvas shoes on the man's feet and realized who it was.

'Bur? I don't understand. Have I been asleep?'

Bur squatted down beside him in the shadows. 'You can call it what you want – you've been in a different time, perhaps.'

'But how did I escape?'

'You had this.'

Gently, Bur prised his hands apart and they both stared down. *Pale grey bark, the colour of ash*, thought Edward. The great tree breaking up, the desolate icy sea, the writhing serpent, were dream pictures that were already fading from his mind, but the branch that he'd struggled through nightmare to retrieve was solid and real.

'Will it do for a tiller?' he asked hesitantly, rubbing his stiff back.

'It will do very well.' Bur's teeth gleamed in a smile; vitality sparkled from him.

'You look different!' said Edward, bemused.

'But of course – you've found *Ringhorn* for me. In truth, you've given me back my soul, and no words can thank you for that.' Bur stood up and held out a hand. 'I want you to see something before it's dark.'

Edward, clutching the branch with his other hand, was pulled to his feet. 'But the tower will be locked by now!' he said in alarm.

But Bur was impatient, already striding across the first floor. Sunset lit the narrow windows, but the empty chambers were dark and they had to feel their way to the main door.

It was too dark to see what Bur did to the padlock. Something clicked and the door swung open, and there was another click as he shut it behind them.

'Wicked!' said Edward. He cast a last wondering look up at the tower, but already it seemed to hide its secrets in the dusk.

Bur had crossed the bridge and was striding over the mound, his head flung back, his tall figure dark against the glowing sky; and his steps were sure as if he knew exactly where he was going. Far away, something exploded against the pink-streaked clouds and, looking up, Edward saw a shower of tiny sparks drift on the breeze. The Carnival fireworks had begun.

They reached the creek; it was low tide. The birds were silent, the marshes empty and quiet, though in the distance Edward could hear the muffled screech and bang of fireworks. Around them the tall grasses gleamed a bright yellow, ripples drifted like gold coins on the surface of the water where it touched the mud, and further away the river was molten with light. The dying sun gilded everything around them except for the wreck of the little boat, which lay in the shadow of the dyke.

As he saw it, Edward felt all his old doubts return. He looked at Bur's face, expecting to see his own feelings mirrored there, but Bur seemed absorbed in his thoughts. He held out his hand for the branch without speaking. Edward gave it to him, and as it passed from his hand into Bur's, he felt suddenly as if the summer evening was charged with something beyond his understanding. Everything around him – the reeds, the long line of the dyke, the rippled water – was stilled but aware.

Bur walked over the mud to the boat. He bent and fitted the branch into the tiller socket and it slipped in easily. Then he stood back under the dyke below Edward. 'Can you see her?'

Edward stared out at the boat's ruined shape, lying in the shadow. Disappointment filled his throat. 'What am I supposed to see?'

'It'll be hard for you. But you've always seen what others haven't. Look – look as you've never looked before.'

Edward looked. He stared until his eyes began to water with the low sun, until the river burned against his vision, until shapes shimmered and danced and were unrecognizable; and the evening was alive and quivered about him, so that each particle of air shone like a tiny lamp. Then, at last, he saw something.

She was bigger than he expected, much bigger. She rose up into the light, a golden prow transparent as glass; but she was only a bright blur on the brighter background of the river, and he wasn't certain if he really saw anything or not. For a second the air was filled with a humming that seemed to come from the ship herself; the prow pulsed with it; then the golden light dissolved and was swallowed up in the small black hulk that was the wreck of the rowing-boat.

'I did see her! I saw something!'

Bur climbed up the dyke beside him; he had brought the branch back. 'Take this home with you. We must both go now.'

'What about—' Edward looked down at the boat. 'Will Locke know we've found her?'

'He can do nothing about *Ringhorn* now. We have a tiller. But it's best you keep it.' Bur looked away, over the marshes, and Edward couldn't see his face. 'I never know what's going to happen to me.'

He began to walk rapidly down the dyke path towards the grit road. Over the black rooftops of Uffenham a million coloured stars were falling, and the moon was rising over the sea.

Edward started after him, holding the branch awkwardly. He wondered how to put his vital question. Bur seemed suddenly so aloof and majestic, he hardly knew him.

'The Newnes sisters said if I found *Ringhorn*, you'd take me to your island for a visit.' He added as firmly as he could, 'We made a bargain.'

Bur glanced down at him. His expression was grim and Edward's heart sank. 'It's not a place for you.'

'But I've seen it! It looks so beautiful!'

The young man's face softened. 'It is. If there was an agreement, it must be kept.'

'So we'll sail in *Ringhorn*?'

'Only I sail *Ringhorn*. Alone.'

At his words Edward's vision of sailing behind that heroic prow to rescue Dad was shattered for ever. Bitterness choked him like dust.

'It cannot be,' Bur said more gently, looking at his face. 'She's part of me and her power's too great. You'd not survive a journey in her.' He touched Edward's arm as if asking for forgiveness. 'Isn't there any other boat?'

'We can take my uncle's, I suppose,' muttered Edward.

'Then I'll find you tomorrow morning.'

From misery he lurched dizzily to joy. 'Tomorrow?'

But Bur was already far away down the dyke path. He seemed to glide along on the last rays of the setting sun, and Edward had to shield his eyes to watch him go.

CHAPTER SIXTEEN

Perilous Voyage

'You *must* be hungry,' said Matt, watching Edward sort gingerly through the kitchen bin.

'What?'

'Try the fridge. It's usually fresher in there.'

'I've lost something, dummy.'

Perhaps Fen had thrown the message away, after all, Edward thought in despair. She was still out at some party for the Carnival Committee and since he'd returned he'd virtually ransacked the kitchen, finishing with the bin. She wasn't into recycling like Mum, and leftover food, rotting cardboard boxes and smeary bottles were all jumbled together.

Matt wrinkled his nose. 'Better get that lot back in before Fen sees it all over the floor. She'll go ballistic.' He didn't offer to help. However, perhaps Edward's dejection was palpable, as a moment later he added cheerily, 'Hodder and I are taking *Freya* out again tomorrow. Why don't you come this time?'

'What?' said Edward, dropping the rotten tomato he had been holding delicately between thumb and forefinger.

Matt began to repeat his invitation patiently, but before he could finish there was the sound of the front door opening. Edward grabbed some kitchen roll and mopped up the mess of tomato, spilt peas and custard on the floor. He had squashed the bin lid down on his leaking parcel by the time Fen sailed through in her black batik dress and red boots, followed by a sheepish-looking Uncle Hodder, clutching half a bottle of wine.

She must have had a good party because she didn't notice the drips running down the bin. But she did take in Edward's anguished face.

'You washed my jeans,' he blurted out.

'You look as if I've committed some heinous crime,' she protested, laughing. 'They were stiff with mud!'

'There was a bit of paper in the pocket. Did you see it?' He was appalled to see a blank look spread across her face. 'You did something with it, didn't you? Please, you must remember!'

'It's been a busy day,' she said, and sank down in mock weariness at the table. 'Don't worry, Ed. It will turn up, I'm sure. What about you boys getting supper? There's cold chicken and salad in the fridge.'

Edward was too worried to give the business

of eating his usual attention. The others seemed inordinately cheerful as they finished the wine and started to clear away.

'Can these go?' said Uncle Hodder, lifting Fen's jar of wilting plants from the middle of the table.

'Chuck 'em, and good riddance,' said Fen, with satisfaction. A brighter gleam had come into her bright eyes.

She was already dreaming of new paintings, thought Edward, new journeys to new places. He looked with sudden sympathy at his uncle, but his uncle was looking at the centre of the table where the jam jar had sat. 'What's this?' he said.

In the circular imprint in the tablecloth was a piece of paper, its creases neatly ironed out by the weight of the jar.

The Parade was very quiet early the next morning as Edward started off for the sailing club. *Everyone must be having a Sunday lie-in after the Carnival* he thought. He'd heard the jangly funfair music until late last night. But now even the tiny waves brushing the shingle were soundless. The only noise was made by a seagull creaking over his head on heavy wings. The sun gleamed behind a white haze that blurred the horizon. There was no wind. Would they ever manage to sail as far as the island?

But at least he had a boat.

Lyddie had sounded puzzled when Edward had phoned her to ask if he could borrow *Widgeon*, the little dinghy that belonged to her and Daniel. He'd said, 'Matt and my uncle are taking *Freya*, and I don't want to go with them' – but he hadn't been able to explain why, or ask Lyddie to crew for him.

He tried to forget her hurt voice as he went into the clubhouse to leave some of his kit – his towel, a change of dry clothes and his jacket – in one of the lockers. The message was in his jacket pocket, which was roomier and safer than the pocket in his shorts. He couldn't bear to lose it again. He'd expected to see Bur by now, but when he arrived Bur hadn't been outside in the dinghy park, where junior members were rigging their boats ready for the Lapwing race, so the message would have to wait until he and Bur arrived back from the island.

Bur still hadn't arrived by the time Edward had rigged *Widgeon*. She was old and heavy and inclined to ship water, and he hoped she'd make it as far as the island. He stood disconsolately watching the other children busy with their Lapwings, longing for Bur's tall figure to appear.

But somehow it happened that one moment Edward couldn't see Bur at all, the next he was at his side; and suddenly the day was lit with gladness.

* * *

Out on the river, there was so little wind that the mainsail hung from the mast like a handkerchief on a stick. As he held the slack jib sheet, Edward worried that they would never reach the river mouth and the sea. Perhaps they'd spend all day drifting with the current and end up on the mud.

Bur had been silent since they'd set off, and Edward felt shy about disturbing him. It didn't seem possible to talk about ordinary, everyday things. But at last the silence between them became too much, and in desperation he came out with, 'I've hidden the branch like you said.'

'This'll end the way it's meant to end, no matter what,' said Bur absently, one hand resting on the motionless tiller. He was looking over at the Martello tower, rising dark against the pearly sky, and the three figures watching them from the mound. It gave Edward an odd, spooky feeling when he realized they were the Newnes sisters. They were always around, he thought, when anything was about to happen. He waved, but they didn't wave back.

'I'll be leaving in *Ringhorn* at first light tomorrow,' Bur said. 'Bring the branch then.'

'But how can we launch her, just the two of us?'

'We'll manage.'

Edward stared ahead at where the lighter Lapwings were twisting and turning across the river like the little birds they were named after. There was a lump in his throat. Bur was leaving because he, Edward, had found *Ringhorn*. There would be nothing to do any more, no one to go and see; only Mae, and she was an old, old lady.

Edward could still see the Newnes sisters watching, the pale blurs of their faces turned to the river, as he and Bur moved away into the haze. For that was what was happening now. There was still no wind, but *Widgeon* had picked up speed somehow. When they went about, he realized that they had left the red sails of the Lapwings behind, that they were past the moored boats, they were running alongside the shingle spit that went on and on until it reached the bar and the open sea.

'We're caught in the tide! We'll have to row all the way back if we're not careful.'

'The wind will come,' said Bur easily. He stretched out his long legs and sat back against the stern, as if prepared to wait for ever. He was relaxed, and it was Edward who was nervous. The summer haze had turned to thick mist as they travelled down river. It was as if *Widgeon* pushed through a circle of light; beyond the circle was a whiteness that hid both banks. He had no idea how close they were to the mud on either side or how near the sea.

'We won't be able to see other boats sailing down on us. Is it safe to go on?'

'Safe?' Bur looked at him, amused. 'You think this journey is safe?'

He swallowed. 'But Locke isn't following us, is he?'

'Locke's everywhere,' said Bur, in a matter-of-fact way. 'You never know where he is, or what secrets he's heard.'

'Like a master spy, you mean? But how does he do it?'

'He's a shape-shifter. He can swim the sea like a fish, or crawl on insect legs through the earth. He can part the air with his wings, like a seagull. He uses all the elements. You can only escape Locke in other ways.'

Edward felt a clutch of fear. He looked at the foaming water rushing beneath the hull, at the silent mist surrounding them. He looked at Bur, so relaxed against the stern, but his eyes bleak and watchful as he gazed ahead. 'What ways?'

'That's what I've got to find out. I did know once, a long time ago.' Bur looked at Edward and his expression softened. 'When we get to the island, it's best you stay in the boat and keep out of harm.'

'But what will you do?'

'I won't be long – as long as it takes to tell my kin I'll return tomorrow.'

Edward tried to keep his dismay to himself. He'd thought that Bur would want to spend some time there, giving him, Edward, plenty of opportunity to nip off in his absence and search for Dad. He stared into the mist, agonizing about how he'd manage it.

The mist was like cold white dust. It frightened him the way it clung round the boat, dampened his hair and furred his sweater. It reminded him of the mist round the great winter tree and what had coiled in the icy sea. And all the time *Widgeon* was being pulled inexorably on through the water.

'We can turn back now,' said Bur gently, seeing his face. 'If that's what you want.' He grinned. 'You're right about rowing back, though!'

The mist slid between Edward's lips. 'No, we must keep on.'

He told himself, *I'm going to find Dad. I'll find a way to do it. That's why I've got to get to the island.*

But what, a tiny voice said, and it was getting louder all the time, *what if he's not there? That means he's dead, dead, DEAD. You know he's not there, you know he's dead, don't you? That's why you haven't told Bur or the Newnes sisters why you want to visit the island. You're frightened they'll say the same. After all, you know in your heart that you can't make him alive just by wanting it badly enough.*

Bur saw him shivering and pulled open the locker under the stern. He took something from the leather rucksack he had brought with him. 'Put this on.'

It was an odd garment, a huge, enveloping cape made of some sort of sacking, and lined with a pungent-smelling, grey and white fur, but Edward obeyed, glad to cover his cold legs. When he pulled the fur-lined hood up, it seemed to keep the taunting voice out. Bur was putting on a similar garment. 'Crude by your standards, but warm. Now try to sleep.'

'Sleep?' he said, astonished.

'We've a long way to go.'

'But you won't be able to sail over the bar single-handed!'

'I've spent an eternity on the sea. Trust me.'

The cape and hood were warm and comforting and Edward's eyes felt gritty with tiredness. He'd hardly slept the previous night for excitement and nerves. He gave in, handed the jib sheet to Bur and slid down into the hull. It was soothing to close his eyelids against the pressing whiteness of the mist, to breathe in the hood's smoky animal smell and rest his cheek against its coarse fur. Just as he was drifting off, he heard Bur begin to sing softly to himself.

Bur was happy, he thought in sleepy surprise. But of course he was. He was going home. Only a short visit this time, but soon he'd be back for ever, sailing there in *Ringhorn*.

* * *

When he awoke, hours seemed to have passed. He thought he'd woken several times during that great long sleep and seen strange things: vast slabs of black rock glistening with ice that rose from the sea; shoals of fish with shining scales like crystal; a huge white bird that perched for a moment on the side of the boat. But perhaps they had all been dreams. He sat up with difficulty because the boat was heeled over, and pulled the hood from his face; with a shock he saw that the exposed fur was powdered with frost.

They were out at sea, so far out he could see no land behind them, just the wash left by the boat, fanning out dark as ink into darker waves. Though the mist had disappeared, there was no sun. The air seemed to pierce his cheeks with cold as it rushed by; the sails were puffed and straining, and where they had been wet with mist were now sharded with icicles.

He turned to see where they were heading and gave a gasp that almost froze his lungs. 'Look, *look*!'

'I've been looking,' shouted Bur above the wind, 'all the time you've been asleep!'

It was land, lighter in colour than the sea, and solid, far away now but drawing closer all the time as *Widgeon* flew like a bird towards it. It was mountainous, Edward could see that, and some of the mountains had strange flat tops as if they had once been – perhaps still were – volcanic. High up, the mountainsides gleamed with snow; the lower slopes were covered by black patches that he thought might be forests. It was impossible to see any houses from this distance.

'Welcome to my island!' shouted Bur.

'It looks so big!' Edward shouted back. He thought, *However will I find Dad there?* 'And we've come so far! I can't believe you swam all the way to Uffenham!'

'The sea's a second element for all my countrymen. We've a sort of power over it.' Bur narrowed his eyes into the distance, where cliffs with the dull sheen of alabaster reared on the horizon. 'I hope I remember where the harbour lies! I feel I've been a lifetime away!'

As they raced nearer, Edward saw that the cliffs were only white because of a thin sprinkling of snow; in the fissures and holes the snow hadn't reached, they were dark iron-grey. They towered above *Widgeon*; craning his head back to look up, he felt tiny and threatened. He clutched *Widgeon*'s side and felt her frailty; a matchstick boat on the black racing water.

'But the island looked so beautiful from far away!'

He didn't think he could be heard above the roaring of the wind and the creaking of the sails, but Bur yelled, 'It is, when the sun's out!' He gestured at the waves spuming white and angry through jagged gaps in the base of the cliffs. 'We don't want to get any closer. We're changing course. Take the jib sheet, can you?'

The jib sheet was a straining, mad thing. Edward pulled on it with all his strength, but his hands were numb.

'Winch her in!' shouted Bur. He held the mainsail sheet in his teeth and helped Edward, then he pulled in the mainsail and faced the waves, his hood blown back, his hair streaming in the wind, his face alight.

Edward's eyes stung and watered so that he could hardly see. His own hood was pulled from his head with the force of the wind, and he felt the cold rake his scalp. As *Widgeon* drove through the waves, icy spray showered his face and made him gasp. He crouched miserably in the bows, as low as he could for protection, more frightened than he'd ever been in his life. This was why he hated sailing! And there was a madman at the helm!

From time to time, Bur shouted orders which he obeyed as best he could, hardly daring to move from his position in case his weight sent *Widgeon* heeling right over and capsizing. He could feel and hear the water surging under the hull, a suffocating, wet blackness beneath them, infinitely deep.

Then at last he heard Bur cry, 'Ready about,' and as he jerked the jib sheet free of the winch and the jib sail billowed round to the other side, he realized they were in calmer water. He blinked the seawater from his eyes and sat up gingerly.

'We're here,' said Bur.

CHAPTER SEVENTEEN
Ice Boy

They were in a sheltered bay, wide and round, as if a bite had been taken out of the coastline. Behind them the cliffs drew together like teeth; before them the land was flat and dark until it reached the mountains, except where it was dappled with snow, or shadowed by spindly trees. They were approaching an empty quay, with the sea licking at its rough stone sides. A huge rectangular building, which Edward thought was a church, rose beyond it.

There was no father, standing with outstretched arms to welcome him. There were no houses, no people. He was filled with a terrible foreboding. 'Where is everyone?'

Bur laughed. His eyes were shining as he sailed *Widgeon* through choppy little waves towards the quayside. 'It's late. They'll be warming themselves by the fire in the great hall.'

'Where's that?'

Bur nodded at the building, and now they were closer Edward saw that smoke blew sideways from the snow-covered roof and golden light glimmered through narrow windows in the stone walls. His spirits lifted. That's where Dad would be! Or someone who'd come across him!

Then he noticed something else. Standing like a shadow itself in the shadow of the distant mountains was an enormous tree. Its roots were as thick as branches and spanned out through the snow in all directions, reaching even to the great building. The perspective was strange from this distance: it seemed as tall as the tallest mountain and its top was hidden by cloud.

Edward clutched Bur and the boat rocked.

'Steady.'

'That's the tree! The tree I climbed! What's it doing here?'

'It's always been here and always will be. We call it the world tree because it grows through all times and places.'

Bur sailed *Widgeon* as close as he could to the quayside. As they came up under its shadow, they let the sails drop and the little boat bumped gently against the wall. Edward grabbed an iron hoop in the stone and secured *Widgeon*'s painter round it in a bowline. Then he tied the mainsail down on to the boom to stop it flapping.

'That'll do,' said Bur, and he leapt out on to the steps that were hewn in the quayside. 'Stay where you are! I won't be long!' The steps were glazed with ice, but he climbed up swiftly on sure feet, his cape billowing out behind him.

A king, thought Edward, *come back to his country*.

He couldn't see anything, but he could hear: Bur's footsteps crunching away over the snow, silence, then a sudden slice of sound – distant cheering, laughter, a great roar of voices – then silence again, not even a seagull mewling overhead, just the jab, jab, jab of waves at *Widgeon*'s side, making her sway and scrape against the stone.

A cold minute passed. He tensed himself for Bur's return, his limbs tingling with anticipation, ready to jump for the steps as soon as Bur was back in the boat. He had to be brave enough for this. But nothing terrible had happened to Bur, had it? Why should he, Edward, be in any danger here? Another minute, another.

Suddenly, Bur was back, coming down the steps, his face turned toward Edward, glowing with happiness. Then he was swinging into the boat, saying, 'Let's get her sailing,' and beginning to undo the mainsail, his back turned.

Edward poised himself and leapt, rocking the boat violently so that Bur staggered forward against the sail. He almost fell on to the steps and the cape twisted round his trainers. He heard a terrible shout beneath him, as Bur took in what had happened. 'Come back, Edward, come back! I can't help you now!'

His bare hands were bleeding from the ice, but so cold he couldn't feel the pain, as he reached the top of the steps. He couldn't think why Bur hadn't come after him. He stood up giddily and looked down. Bur, in the boat far below, looked up at him.

'I'm sorry, Bur,' he called. 'I have to do it!' But he wasn't sure that he had heard.

A stone causeway led away from the quay to the hall, covered with a thin layer of snow, and crusted with ice and black, wind-blown sand. Where the snow had melted and frozen over again, Edward saw the dark smudges of many feet.

He was trying to hurry in case Bur came after him, and once he stumbled and just stopped himself falling. A thick black root, hidden by snow, one of the roots from the great winter tree, had grown right out here and lay partly under the stones, like a sleeping snake. He took a deep breath of freezing air to steady himself. It would be warm in the hall.

There was a wide wooden door in front of him, set in the stone wall of the building and girded with iron bands. He couldn't see any sort of handle. He knocked timidly. The knock sounded very loud in the silent, snowy world, but nothing happened. Probably they were making too much noise inside to hear him.

How had Bur got in? Edward set his shoulder against the door and pushed. It moved, very slightly. Again, he pushed. The door opened a crack, and through that crack he squeezed.

It was very dark inside, and the air smelt of the freezing depths of the sea. He knew at once that something was wrong. Where was the fire? The candlelight? The people? Was he in some sort of outer room?

He stood trembling while his eyes adjusted to the gloom. Grey light filtered through the narrow windows and after a few panic-stricken seconds he was able to make out long wooden tables, benches, some sort of fabric hanging on the walls. At the far end there was an enormous empty hearth; above him, the beamed roof and the pillars that supported it were in shadow, and in the corners the shadows thickened into darkness. Under the soles of his trainers there was the grit of unswept sand on the stone floor. Roots, like the one he had seen outside, had cracked open the stone in places, had pushed upwards and over the floor like enormous black tentacles, winding themselves round table legs and benches. A powdering of dust lay on the surfaces of the tables and the hangings on the walls held no colour at all.

He didn't understand: this wasn't where Bur had come. There had been noise, the sound of people; he had heard it himself. This place hadn't been inhabited for years.

'Is anybody here?' he said in a cracked voice, his breath white as frost. 'Dad?' he whispered. 'Dad?'

Only a deadening silence, like a tomb.

Edward fell on to a bench and buried his face in his hands. He wanted to weep, but his eyes were so painfully dry the tears couldn't come. He could only sit there; and in his utter desolation, he thought his heart would break.

Through his grief he heard a noise. He looked up sharply, and thought he saw a hanging twitch by the floor, something run out across the floor. A rat?

'Poor Edward,' said Locke's voice. 'You've been cheated, haven't you?'

Edward stared round wildly in the gloom, his heart beating with shock. He couldn't tell where Locke was standing.

'Poor, poor Edward,' said Locke's voice again, and it sounded warm and comforting. 'Bur's cheated you, I'm afraid. He's brought you here as a reward for finding his boat, but what a horrible place it is! You trusted him, but there's nothing – no one – here, is there?'

Edward found his voice. 'How do you know it was – a reward? Did you *spy* on us?'

Locke laughed. 'I can't be everywhere at the right time, Edward, much as I'd like to be. I have to rely on common sense. I realize Bur wouldn't come back for a casual visit, you see. It's dangerous for him to stay ashore too long before his final return. So I'm right – it was a reward for finding *Ringhorn*. But now you find nothing – no one – here.'

'But there were people here, I heard them!' Edward stared warily into the shadows.

'People? My poor boy, this place is empty. I can't think why you wanted to come. What seemed so important about it?' His voice was very soft.

'My father,' whispered Edward. His precious secret was no longer worth keeping. 'He went missing last summer.'

'And you thought you'd find him here? But it's a dead place, Edward. Look about you.'

Locke was right. There was nothing but darkness and dust.

'How did you get here?' asked Edward dully.

'It's easy enough for me.' Locke's voice sounded amused. Edward could imagine his eyes crinkling at the corners. 'I can change shape – fly, swim. If poor Bur had been able to do that, he would never have needed *Ringhorn*, he would never have needed to use you in the way he has.'

Locke was right, Edward thought bitterly.

'I warned you about him, didn't I?' said Locke. 'I said you should let me know if you came across him. I could have warned you about the trickery he'd use to get you to search for his precious boat.'

'It was the Newnes sisters, mostly,' muttered Edward.

Locke laughed again, without mirth. 'Those arch manipulators! You allowed them to work on you, didn't you? They wanted the story to end their way, yet again.'

'What do you mean?'

'They don't like the pattern to have too many variants. That's in case the outcome doesn't work out in the same way it always has done. But they took a terrible risk when they allowed you to come here.'

'Why?' Edward said listlessly.

'Don't you understand, Edward, *you* are the variant this time? You can give me the chance to break free of the pattern – and I can tell you, I'm heartily sick of it.' The weariness in Locke's voice reached Edward dimly. 'If you do, the whole business can finish once and for all.'

Edward's brain felt sluggish with cold. He shook his head to clear it.

'Wouldn't you like to pay those old women back for using you – Bur, too?' said Locke softly.

A sour, cruel little anger twisted inside Edward suddenly, rousing him. 'Pay them back?'

'You have such power, remember? You have the branch from the great ash tree. They don't know where it is. You haven't told Bur, have you?'

'No.'

'Then don't give it to him. He can't return without it. It won't take many days trapped in your world before his strength is sapped again. He and *Ringhorn* will die together. *Ringhorn* is useless without her tiller; Bur will die without *Ringhorn*.'

'You're asking me to *murder* him?'

'You don't have to do anything, that's the point. Go back with him now, but don't take the branch to him for the sailing. Oh, yes, don't look so surprised. I realize he must have planned his escape by now. Don't help him. Destroy the branch. A piece of wood will burn in minutes.'

'I can't do that,' said Edward, in consternation.

'When you say goodbye to Bur today, you'll never have to face him again.'

Edward shook his head. Then as the full horror dawned on him he repeated, 'I can't!' more loudly. He waited, but Locke said nothing more.

He had been too upset before to notice that the pillars supporting the roof were encased in a chrysalis of ice. No wonder it was so cold in here! He must go before he froze to death. It didn't seem that Locke, wherever he was, would prevent him leaving.

Something scratched across the sandy floor. A large grey crab was crawling slowly sideways under the table, its pincers waving. Yes, definitely time to go.

He got up stiffly and stepped away from the table. The pillar nearest him seemed to send out an aura of burning cold that he could feel even through his cape. Where the light fell on it, it glistened like crystal. He put out his hand in wonder.

A prickling sensation, like freezing pins and needles, darted at once through his fingertips. He tried to wrench them away from the ice. But they wouldn't come. They were stuck fast.

He stared in horror at his hand, fingers soldered to the pillar as if they had become part of it. The pins and needles had reached his palm now, were running to his wrist; already he was losing sensation in his fingers.

'I'm sorry, Edward,' said Locke's voice. Nothing moved except the crab, which had climbed on to the surface of the table and was crawling slowly through the dust. 'You're a nice boy, but too nice, I'm afraid. You're going to have to stay here. You see, I don't want Bur to have that branch.'

Edward could feel the ice creeping in his veins. It wasn't painful, but oddly soothing. It deadened everything; he didn't have to feel anything any more. He didn't have to feel the pain of his father's death, the death of his own dreams. This was the way out: to become a pillar of ice for all eternity. No one would ever know that beneath the ice there had once been a living, breathing boy.

There was a sudden scraping sound. The door was being forced further open, letting a spear of daylight into the hall and an icy gust of air. Something stood against the light: a monstrous head, silhouetted. Then a voice.

'Hello, Ed,' said Matt.

CHAPTER EIGHTEEN

Shape-Shifter

Edward didn't want to speak, but some instinct for life, burning deep inside, forced the words out. 'You've got to get me out of this, Matt!'

He couldn't think why or how Matt was here, or why he was wearing the sea god's costume, but his right arm was freezing to the elbow and it wouldn't be long before the numbness reached his heart.

Matt took off his great helmet with its glimmering shells and put it down on the nearest bench. He lumbered over in his sea boots, using his trident for balance but still almost tripping over his cloak and the twisted tree roots. He didn't appear scared or puzzled, but looked around incuriously.

'Help me, for God's sake,' Edward said faintly, to catch his attention. 'I'm stuck. I'm dying, Matt.'

Matt's face didn't change as he took in Edward's hand, drained of colour now, welded to the pillar.

'Hang on,' he said in an odd, calm way. 'Cover your eyes with your other hand.'

Edward obeyed speechlessly. There was a terrific whack above his head. Ice cracked over his shoulders like glass, tinkling on to the floor. Again, *thwack*! Again and again, something heavy and sharp thumped against the pillar and blades of ice fell outwards, exposing the ancient wood.

A final bang and Edward's hand was free. He crouched on the ground nursing it back to life, tucking it inside his cape, under his sweater against the warmth of his chest. As the blood began to circulate again, the excruciating pain brought tears to his eyes at last.

Matt laid the trident down on the table. 'Have their uses, those things,' he remarked casually. He eyed Edward. 'Give me your hand.'

It was the grasp of Matt's warm hand, so positively alive, that finally took the numbness away from Edward's.

Something of the strangeness of it all seemed to be getting through to Matt at last. 'It's cold, isn't it?' he said, with a shudder.

'I thought Dad might be here,' whispered Edward.

Matt's face was strangely without expression and so was his voice as he said, 'You won't find him here, Ed. Not anywhere. Dad's dead. Even in my dreams I know that.'

'I think I knew it too.' Edward paused. 'How did you get here?'

'I walked,' said Matt, in a matter-of-fact way. He stood up and began to clump about in his boots, regarding the pillars blankly.

'Over the *sea*?'

'I'm a sea god.'

'But it's only a costume!'

A small frown of confusion furrowed Matt's brow. 'It doesn't matter,' said Edward. 'The main thing is you got here.' He stood up and rubbed his stiff legs.

At that moment they both heard a sudden clicking sound in the hall. Something moved, not far away. Matt stopped and stared round into the shadows, as if his senses were gradually becoming more alert. Edward stood transfixed, his heart beating faster.

'It's only a crab,' said Matt. Then he saw Edward's face and this time he seemed to take it in properly. 'What's the matter?'

'It's not a crab,' whispered Edward. 'It's a man called Locke. He can change shape, into a crab, into anything. He's dangerous, Matt.'

Matt seemed to accept this information in a most un-Matt-like way. At any other time Edward would have thought it odd. But now he was thankful when he didn't ask any questions, but lumbered over to him as quietly as he could. Without speaking, he gestured at the door.

'If we try to get out, he'll stop us,' said Edward into his ear.

'Simple,' Matt hissed back. 'We'll catch him first!'

They could see the crab, half hidden by a tree root, motionless as if it were waiting for them to act. Grains of black sand stirred as it waved its front legs. Edward didn't like the look of its claws.

'How? We can't catch it with our bare hands!' For a moment he imagined hitting it with the trident – the shell splitting, the squelch of its soft body – and shuddered.

Silently, Matt took off his cloak. Under it he wore his waterproof sailing anorak, an incongruous hot red in the cold grey light of the hall. He was shivering as he held a length of the cloak out to Edward, but Edward understood at once, and gripped it at both ends. The delicate lining of shining, blue-green, silk-like stuff drifted down to the floor and Matt bunched it away under one arm. What he and Edward now held between them was the outer layer of the cloak. On its own it resembled a large fishing net, strongly woven from tough black twine. The little shells and dried silvery fish scales that had decorated it pattered to the floor.

They waited, hardly breathing, for the crab to move, their breath pluming white in the gloom, the net held out in front of them. It was deathly silent; Edward could not even hear the sea.

The crab twitched a front leg, its claw extended. It lurched forward under the root like a tank and out on to the sandy floor. It moved sideways quickly, with a horrible scratching, scrabbling sound that set Edward's teeth on edge, and it was making for the table. It would be difficult to catch it under there. They had to do it now.

Slowly, stealthily, holding the net cloak out by its corners, they advanced.

The crab paused, as if it sensed something happening. Matt nodded to Edward, they both leapt forward and down; and before the crab could escape, they had pinioned it in the net.

Close to, it was a sickening size and the surface of the enormous filth-streaked shell was pitted with holes as if it had been worm-eaten. It was difficult to hold the net safely: the crab's dust-covered legs writhed through the holes; its claws opened and closed within inches of their fingers. Edward couldn't look; he couldn't bear to see the grotesque, fleshy underside. They knelt there for dreadful seconds trying to hold the net to the floor and protect their hands while the thing convulsed beneath it.

At last Matt said, 'It can't get out, Ed! Let's go!'

Edward was about to loosen his numb fingers when the crab changed in front of his eyes. A tail lashed through the net, teeth snapped. Under his grip a great slimy body was flapping about, frantic to get out. In horror he almost let go.

'It's changed into a fish!' he yelled.

Matt was white-faced. He held on grimly while the creature twisted about with enormous strength, glaring at them with round jelly eyes. Edward's fingertips were sticky with the fish's slime; still holding the net, he tried to move them to avoid its snapping jaws. He could see its teeth, pointed and lethal.

'It'll bite through the net! What'll we do, Matt?'

'It'll die in a minute from not being in water. Leave it! Run!'

Their limbs were heavy and stiff with cold. They struggled to their feet and made clumsily for the door, tripping over sprawling roots and benches that lay in the shadows. Matt left his helmet and trident where they were, on the table. Edward's cape caught at a pillar as he passed and he ripped it away, leaving shreds of the coarse material sticking to the ice.

The door was still ajar from Matt's entrance. With relief Edward saw daylight outside, felt colder air against his cheeks. They were almost there when something made him glance back. He gripped Matt's arm. 'Look!'

The giant fish had thrashed or bitten its way out of the net and lay some way from it on the floor. They saw the gleam of the grey scales against the dusty stone, the jerking of its body as the mouth gaped open.

'It's dying,' said Matt, with satisfaction.

Edward gulped. 'It's really a man, Matt.'

Suddenly, there was a flash of white. Something was struggling from the dying fish's jaws, something live and white. The carcass of the fish collapsed, crumbling into the dust of the floor. But the white thing rose into the air with a harsh, yodelling cry and a spread of snowy wings. It circled the hall in a powerful arc, then, as Edward clutched Matt, it came sweeping towards them.

'Look out!' he shouted.

They ducked as the bird dived over their heads, lifting their hair with the speed of its flight. Edward caught a glimpse of a heavy yellow bill that curved into a vicious point before he covered his eyes. Crouched on the floor, he waited for the attack to begin, for the stabs of pain as the terrible beak was driven into him. But all he felt was the bitter draught through the partly open door.

'It's gone,' said Matt. 'Flown up into the roof, I think. Anyway, a seagull can't stop us leaving.'

Trembling, Edward took his hands away from his eyes. There was silence behind them, and shadows. He couldn't see anything. He stood up warily.

Then Locke's voice made him start violently. 'Have you changed your mind yet, Edward?'

'No!' His voice was high-pitched with fear.

'Who are you?' shouted Matt next to him, staring round wildly. 'Come out, wherever you are!'

'He's changed back,' whispered Edward. 'He's changed from the bird into a man again.'

'I can't let you go, Edward. I can't let you take the branch to Bur.' Locke's voice was regretful but cold. 'Are you really willing to face death for someone who has betrayed you?'

'What's he talking about?' hissed Matt. 'Is he mad?'

There was a pause, then the disembodied voice said, almost casually, 'A pity to shed blood in here, but I don't see any alternative.'

The light from outside suddenly dimmed. For a moment Edward thought that Locke had shut the door against them. But there was a thickening of shadow in front of it and a pulse of movement in the shadow as if something vast and powerfully alive was sniffing the air. Hot damp gusts reached him, carrying the sickening stench of blood and undigested meat, and beneath it was a bitter, musky scent.

Something that wasn't human was breathing only a few paces away.

They clung together, trembling. 'Don't move!' whispered Matt.

'It can smell us!'

There was a low rumble by the door and something scratched the stone floor. The beast was shifting position; for a second, grey light showed a long, grizzled flank.

Edward moaned with fear. 'He's a bear, Matt!'

Matt's grip tightened round him. 'There's nothing we can do.'

Edward hid his eyes against Matt's chest; Matt curled himself over Edward.

They waited in terror for the end.

Locke's voice spoke from the shadow. 'There's something Edward can tell me that will save you both.'

It took a moment before they dared let go of each other. Edward was speechless, and Matt had to nudge him. He licked dry lips. *Was the beast still there?*

'Where's the stone, Edward?'

'I haven't got it any more,' he stammered.

'A pity to be so careless with others' belongings,' said Locke's voice. 'Where is it?'

'Tell him, for God's sake!' whispered Matt.

'But I don't know where—'

'Tell him anything!' They stared into the shadows. 'Get rid of that creature first!' Matt shouted out, with great bravado.

There was a pause that seemed endless, then the shadow by the door shrunk in on itself and dull light slid into the hall. The stench was lost in a blast of icy fresh air.

Locke sounded amused. 'You didn't think I wanted to do anything more than frighten you, did you? The cold would have done the rest in due course, anyway. Now, what were you telling me, Edward?'

Resisting the temptation to run, Edward said quickly, 'I threw the stone away in Uffenham, in one of the streets on the hill. I threw it into the garden of an empty house, near a playground.'

Locke didn't answer. They didn't know if he was still in the hall, or if he had already slipped out in another shape through one of the windows.

Matt grabbed Edward's hand. 'Come on, Ed!' They ran across the floor, ducked under the icicles that hung above the doorway and were outside at last.

Edward looked up and thought he saw the great span of a white wing cleaving the sky above him; feathers falling. 'It's snowing!' he gasped, trying to find the stone path through a curtain of drifting flakes.

Matt's grip on his hand was slipping away. He turned in panic, but could see nothing through the steadily falling grey-whiteness. Then he heard Matt's voice, muffled and oddly different.

'You shouldn't have let me sleep!'

Edward stared, puzzled, blinking as snowflakes stuck to his eyelashes. There was a sudden flash as if a photographic slide had been superimposed over the falling dots of white, and he saw two dark figures in a boat against the background of a sunlit riverbank, then it had gone. And so had Matt.

There was only the faint hiss of flakes against his cheek, and the ground was so thick with fresh snow he had no idea where he was, or in which direction lay the quay.

He staggered forward. A dark, moving rectangle gleamed in front of him. Water. The snowflakes changed pattern, fanning out over a stony ridge. And below him on the water was a darker shape. He had reached the quay and the boat. And Bur.

He crouched, numb fingers fumbling along the edge for the steps. Then somehow he was clambering down, his cape heavy with ice splinters, and below him in the lurching boat Bur held out his arms towards him.

Edward ignored him. As he reached the bottom of the steps, he leapt for the boat through the falling snow. His feet slipped on wood; he was falling back in a tangle of cape and limbs. Something hard and heavy hit him across the forehead and the white flakes went black.

CHAPTER NINETEEN

Back to the Beginning

'Are you awake?' Bur's face was close to his, the eyes very blue and gentle.

Edward blinked. There was late afternoon sun on his face, and salt from a faint breeze. The boat creaked comfortably round him and under him the wooden planks were hard.

Gingerly, he put a hand to his head. His hood had gone; he was no longer wearing the fur-lined cape. There was no bump on his forehead, none in his hair either, but it felt different: stiff and windswept, as if it had survived a perilous journey, but only just.

'The boom hit me, didn't it?' he muttered, but when he sat up, he saw they were sailing down the river, and it was in bright focus, sparkling in the sunshine. The mist had disappeared. 'I must have been knocked out for hours!' Yet he felt well, not muzzy as if he'd been concussed.

The breeze was pushing them downriver without effort and in the far distance Edward could already see the Martello tower and beyond it the sailing club. Bur's eyes were on the mainsail and he let it out further.

'I don't understand anything,' said Edward. 'There were people in the hall when you were in it. But when I arrived it was empty.'

'It only lives when I'm there.'

'I thought my father was there.' Edward looked across the bright water and it suddenly blurred. 'He didn't come back from a sailing trip last summer.' He wiped his eyes with the back of his hand.

'He's gone to his own island,' said Bur gravely, still watching the sail, 'and you can't follow him there. You must let him go, Edward. You've your own life to live, here and now.'

There was a long silence between them. The river rippled softly away beneath the boat and Edward thought about his father and about himself. It was hard not to cry with the pain in his chest, but he couldn't do it in front of Bur.

After a while, he managed to say, 'Locke was there, in your hall. He wanted to stop me bringing you the branch tomorrow morning.'

'And will you bring it?'

Edward shrugged. 'I suppose.'

He had found *Ringhorn* for Bur because he'd

thought he would find his father by doing so. There was nothing in it for him, not any more. But if he didn't bring the branch, Bur would die, and his island with him.

'If Matt hadn't come into the hall, I might have frozen to death.' He frowned. 'How was Matt there, on the island?'

'The fates sent him a dream. I couldn't come and rescue you myself, you see.'

Edward looked at Bur sitting peacefully by the helm, outlined by sunlight. 'Locke wants you to die, you know,' he blurted out. 'He threatened me because of it.'

'I know,' said Bur calmly.

'But why? Why does he hate you so much?'

'Because I am what I am, and he is what he is.'

'He's evil, isn't he? But *why*?'

'That's the way he's chosen.'

They were sliding between the moored boats in front of the clubhouse. Bur called, 'Ready about!' and Edward took the other sheet as the jib came round. There was no time for talking as they came up to the jetty head to wind and let the mainsail flap.

A small group of children stood on the sunlit slipway. A boy came to help with *Widgeon*, taking the painter from Edward and attaching it to a bollard while Edward stood in the bows and pulled the jib down.

'Where's your trolley?' said the boy.

'Thanks, but it's OK,' said Edward. 'My friend'll help me get it.' He turned from securing the halyard to the mast and looked round the ballooning mainsail. 'Bur?'

There was no golden figure in the stern. While Edward had had his back to him pulling the jib down, he must have stepped lightly out of *Widgeon* on to the jetty, and left.

Everyone was in the tiny kitchen at Gull Cottage when he arrived back: Matt eating cake at the table, Uncle Hodder making tea and Fen washing her brushes at the sink.

'You've been ages,' she snapped. Her dark hair stuck up, looking bristly and cross. 'And you forgot your picnic!' She pointed accusingly at a plastic bag bulging on the floor.

'I'll eat it now,' said Edward obligingly. He felt famished now that he'd been reminded he'd had no lunch.

She snorted. 'Look at the clock! It's almost suppertime! You had me wondering where you'd got to – not worrying, mind you, just wondering. It was quite misty when you started.' She looked so upset still that Edward mumbled, 'Sorry,' wondering suddenly if she'd thought he'd drowned, like Dad.

'I suppose you dreamt the afternoon away like your brother!'

He shot a startled glance at Matt, who nodded ruefully. 'I dozed off for a bit after we'd moored and had our picnic. Long enough for Hodder to let us get stuck on the mud!'

'I did try to wake you,' protested Uncle Hodder, 'but you were so deeply asleep it seemed a shame. It was really quite pleasant being stranded there in the sun, doing nothing except watch the moorhens.' He smiled his gentle smile.

Fen brandished a paintbrush at Edward. 'Lyddie came round to see if you were back. I suspect she feels that now Daniel's friend is leaving you won't pay her much attention in future.'

'So Patrick's going, is he?' said Edward slowly. *Maybe I'll drop round at Daniel's tomorrow*, he thought.

'Don't forget Lyddie now. She was upset you didn't ask her sailing today. And it was her boat!'

'I'll make it up to her,' said Edward. He meant it.

Matt winked, and pushed the cake towards him. 'What's this?' he breathed. 'Can it be – Romance?'

'Your Vali's been round, too,' said Fen dryly. 'I didn't get much painting done this afternoon, what with chatting to those girlfriends of yours, and taking the costumes up to the Drama Club. At least I've got them out of the way now . . .' she paused, '. . . except

226

yours, Matt. What happened to the sea god costume?'

'Haven't a clue,' said Matt, eating cake and looking unconcerned. 'I left it with the rest of the things.'

'I suppose someone from the float took a fancy to it,' said Fen. 'Pity. It was so magnificent.'

'It was magic,' said Matt, and for a second a strange expression flickered across his face.

Exhaustion overcame Edward soon after that. His limbs felt so leaden, he could hardly lift his fork to his mouth at supper.

'Bed!' Fen said afterwards, and he didn't protest.

The back bedroom was flooded with evening sun. He went straight over to his bed and pulled back the duvet. The branch lay in the dip in the middle of the mattress, the sheet beneath it smeared with wood grain. At least this would be the last night he'd have to share his bed with such a hard object.

As he drew the curtains he stared out at the sea, screwing up his tired eyes against the golden light. The long clouds that shadowed the evening sky were reflected in the sea, but the horizon was empty. Would the island ever show itself to him again, now?

'You'll be back there tomorrow, Bur,' he whispered. 'Wherever it is, you'll be back.'

'Dig a hole, deep as hell, and never, NEVER tell! But you did tell, Edward! You told him where you'd thrown the mistletoe stone!'

Hours later, it seemed, Mae's voice woke him.

Without opening his eyes he mumbled, 'I had to tell him. It was to save Matt and me!' But the sound he was making was a string of gibberish. He was still half asleep, and it was an effort to open his eyes.

Mae's round, powdery face was peering down into his sorrowfully, and that was all he could see, though he was aware of sunlight around her and warmth on the back of his head. He pushed the duvet back from his shoulders, and tried to make her understand. 'I'm sorry—'

Something had happened to his speech.

The shock made him try to sit up but someone or something was sitting heavily on his legs at the end of the bed. He couldn't move.

A shadow fell across him. 'You must watch now,' said Astrid sternly. 'You must see what you have done by saving your own skin.'

'Sisters, you are forgetting,' said a softer voice. Zelma put a cool hand on his forehead and his panic subsided. He turned his head on the pillow and looked up into her face. It was as gentle as he remembered it, but seemed frailer, more darkly shadowed. 'What has happened – is about to happen – is not Edward's fault. We can only work for the right outcome of the story.'

'I'm sorry, child,' whispered Mae. 'We've brought you back to the beginning, so you understand.' A tear rolled down her cheek, washing a path through the powdery wrinkles. Bewildered, Edward squinted at her against the sun, wondering why she was crying. Astrid said nothing, but her face worked fiercely and she too had the glitter of tears in her eyes.

Then suddenly they had left his bedside. He raised his head from the pillow and blinked.

He was lying in bed in the middle of a vast sunny meadow.

He knew where he was at once. He could see snow-capped mountains in the distance, and beyond the waving grasses and blue flowers of the meadow, the hall, with its door open wide to let in the sunlight. There were bright leaves on the great ash tree and its branches reached up through a cloudless sky. Its roots were everywhere, as if the tree was the living framework that held this green summer world together. Sitting snugly between two roots was a small cottage Edward recognized.

There was no time to puzzle out what the Newneses' cottage was doing here. People were emerging from a distant glade of little silver trees. To his astonishment he suddenly heard someone say his uncle's name.

Was it his uncle? Edward frowned against the sunlight. The man's eyes seemed very dark. Perhaps

229

Uncle Hodder was wearing his sunglasses. Someone was holding his arm, guiding him, as if the light was too dazzling. With a shock Edward saw it was Bur. Neither of them noticed Edward lying in bed a short distance away; no one seemed to see him at all.

Now they had formed a circle with Bur in the middle. Men and youths began to move round him in a slow, rhythmic dance. They were close enough for Edward to make out stones, twigs and clods of earth in their hands, as if they'd collected them under the trees. To his horror he saw a youth drew back his hand and hurl a stick at Bur's back. Strangely, Bur didn't cry out or turn.

They were taking turns to throw. A stone struck Bur's cheek but it didn't bleed. Sticks and pebbles bounced off him and fell to the grass, and each time the men laughed. Their laughter wasn't cruel or taunting. They didn't want to hurt Bur, thought Edward, in relief. It was only a game. He could see Bur, invincible in the centre of the dark, dancing figures, smile back at them. Uncle Hodder stood awkwardly outside the circle, looking as if he didn't understand what was going on at all.

Someone was approaching Edward's bed. It was the long, lithe strides Edward recognized first, then the burnished hair. He kept still, hardly breathing while Locke sat down on a tree root in the sun. He didn't appear to see the bed or Edward himself peering out from under his duvet in terror.

Locke's hair burned against the green grass, and he was whistling between his sharp white teeth as he chipped away at something with a knife. The blade scraped on wood. *I've seen that plant in his hand before*, thought Edward. *White berries, like blind eyes*.

Locke ripped the berries off and they fell on the grass, bruised and oozing. He sharpened the end of the stem into a point, an arrowhead. The birdsong died as he jumped to his feet, the movement rocking Edward's bed so violently it seemed Locke had the power to move the earth.

Shouting Hodder's name, Locke ran across the meadow with the mistletoe dart in his hand. When he lifted his head, Edward saw that he and Uncle Hodder were talking together.

There was a gap in the circle of dancers and they moved into it. He saw Bur smile at the new players. Locke put Hodder's hand over the dart, away from the sharp end, then he put his own hand over Hodder's. Hodder stood patiently, waiting for his turn to throw.

Locke's tricked him, thought Edward. *He doesn't realize it's a weapon!*

He struggled to get out of bed, but something was still holding his legs down. A thick black root from

231

the jigsaw tree had grown like a tentacle over his bed, right over his legs. He tried to kick it off, but it seemed to tighten. He couldn't move.

Then Locke drew Hodder's hand back to throw. Far away the first golden leaf of autumn drifted down from the great ash tree, and Bur turned his head to watch it. The deadly dart was black against the sun, poised for flight.

'No!' Edward shouted. 'Bur! Bur!'

But he made no sound.

CHAPTER TWENTY

The Night Walkers

With a gasp, Edward opened his eyes. He lay, his heart pounding, in the darkness of the back bedroom, listening to the deep silence in the cottage. There was *still* something across his legs. The branch had somehow fallen sideways under the duvet. He jerked his legs free and drew them up to his chest for comfort while his heartbeat slowed and his breathing became normal.

What had he seen? He could only think that Bur must be in terrible danger. He had to warn him.

Shivering, he scrambled into his clothes as fast as he could; it was surprisingly cold in the bedroom. The floor creaked as he stood up, but there was still no sound from Matt, no breathing, even.

Puzzled, Edward went over to Matt's bed. The duvet was humped up but there was no one in it. Matt must have gone dawn fishing, as he sometimes did. But in the middle of the night?

Edward dragged the branch out from under his own duvet and, steadying it against himself, went out on to the landing. Past the silent second bedroom. Then softly down the stairs, trying to prevent the branch banging against the curve in the staircase. There was a light on in the hall and a cold draught blowing in under the front door.

He rested the branch against the wall, grabbed his jacket from its peg and threw it on. Matt's jacket had gone and the bolt on the front door had been drawn back. The latch was down, reminding Edward to put the spare house key into one of his pockets. Then he picked up the branch and clicked the door shut behind him.

He stood uncertainly in the chilly, yellow-lit High Street while he manoeuvred the branch into position: the easiest way to carry it seemed to be over his shoulder like a rifle. There were footsteps coming along the street towards him, people who might wonder what he was doing out alone at this hour. Hastily, he slipped down the side street at the corner of Gull Cottage, into Marine Street, turning towards Neptune Alley.

The Carnival bunting made shadowy patterns over the quiet pavements. There were no lights in the windows. He'd forgotten to look at the clock to see what time it was, and he wasn't wearing his watch.

He was glad of his jacket as it was amazingly cold; the air felt almost frosty in his nostrils, the stinging, vibrant, clean cold that doesn't belong to a summer night.

Marine Street had fewer lampposts than the High Street, but as Edward passed under the first one he saw tiny particles falling slowly through the golden beam above him, glittering and turning as they fell. At first he thought they were moths dazzled by the light, but they weren't; they were snowflakes, and in the light he could see them spangling the sleeves of his jacket before dissolving into dark pinheads. He felt them touch his face like feathers, brush against his lips.

All around him, snow was falling, softly, lightly, through the night.

Perhaps it was the strange spectacle of summer snow that was bringing people outside, away from their warm beds, because Marine Street seemed to be full of footsteps suddenly, clanging and echoing down the pavements that hadn't yet been covered by snow. He had to dodge into the shadows to avoid being seen. A family – mother, father, with two small children, impeccably behaved – walked hand in hand. Next, an older couple. Then a group of youths and girls. They were coming towards him, but no one was talking, even in whispers. They didn't appear to notice Edward, but after they had passed he quickened his pace, the branch thumping against his shoulder.

Neptune Alley was a tunnel of darkness. He had to feel his way along the snow-wet walls, searching for the gap made by the arch.

It wasn't there.

He checked again, running his fingers along the painted brickwork. The alleyway was merely a gap between the windowless walls of the houses on either side. He almost tripped over a clump of grass and gasped as he touched something damp and silky: a pale hollyhock sprawled against one wall.

But the cottage belonging to the Newnes sisters had vanished.

It's gone back to the island where it belongs, and they've gone with it, thought Edward, trembling with shock and cold. Then Bur would be impatient to get back to the island himself. Perhaps he'd already be waiting by the boat.

He turned and blundered back the length of Neptune Alley, his feet slipping in the snow. He burst out of the darkness into the street light, and stopped.

The scattered walkers had become a crowd. While he had been in Neptune Alley he hadn't heard their footsteps: the snow which lay in a light, gleaming powder over the street muffled any sound. But in any case the crowd moved without speaking, eyes fixed on some point ahead. They were wearing only their nightclothes – a motley assortment of striped and plain pyjamas and nighties in brushed nylon, bright florals or much-washed cotton – with their coats and jackets pulled hastily on top, as if they were taking part in an unexpected fire practice.

A man passed Edward in a mackintosh neatly belted and buttoned, the effect rather spoiled by the flapping pale-blue nightshirt he wore underneath, which exposed thin, hairy ankles and fat, hairy slippers. He thought he recognized the man from the hotel whom he'd spoken to one evening about the island. Timidly, he pulled the mackintosh sleeve.

'Excuse me, sir. Where's everyone going?'

The man looked at him and the branch with an incurious gaze and didn't answer, continuing on with the crowd. Everyone was walking at the same pace through the thin, softly falling snow – steadily and oddly purposeful, as if summoned by a call Edward could not hear.

I'll go on to the Parade, he thought uneasily. *At least I'll avoid them there.*

It was a shock to find the Parade more crowded than Marine Street. With enormous relief he saw someone he knew.

'Lyddie!' He shouted her name, pushed through people, until he was at her side. 'Lyddie! Am I glad to see you! What's going on?'

She looked pale, gazing ahead with a little frown between her eyes. She'd put her glasses on, though, and an oversized jacket that must belong to Daniel.

'Lyddie!' He danced in front of her to catch her attention, jigging the branch up and down. 'Remember me?' It was no good. She was looking straight through him, ignoring him. She must still be upset that he hadn't asked her sailing. 'Look, I'm sorry about yesterday—'

But the crowd had swept her away.

'Lyddie!' he yelled. The snow whispered in his ears, and to his left, below the Parade, the dark waves sighed over the shingle. The great sea of people drew together round him, moving on inexorably; and nobody spoke a word.

He let himself be caught up by the crowd. He had no choice: sooner or later uncaring, marching feet would trample him down. At least he was being carried along in the right direction – to the end of the Parade and the last houses, towards the marshes and the river.

The silent crowd suddenly reminded Edward of Matt, the night he'd taken the mistletoe stone and sleepwalked on to the landing. These people were all sleepwalking. The dark rolling sea, the lamp-lit snow, gleaming white in the cold black summer's night, might all be part of a dream. But he knew he was awake: the branch was digging into his shoulder.

And he wasn't the only one, after all. The figures on either side of him, a girl and a youth, had turned and were staring down at him, their very wide-awake eyes hard and triumphant. And a third figure, a boy, was blocking his way, causing chaos in the crowd.

Locke's children had found him.

'Edward?' said Helga, and she smiled and flung back her long dark hair so that strands of it whipped his cheek. 'You've got something my father wants.' She reached for the branch.

'No!' He ducked away from her and found his face jammed into the leather jacket that belonged to the swarthy young man on his other side. His teeth were bared in an unpleasant leer.

'Get the branch, Wolf!' cried Helga.

Edward tried to run but the third figure was waiting. The spindly boy called Snick snaked out an arm and curled it round the branch. 'You heard her. Our dad wants this.'

'He can't have it!' panted Edward, trying to twist it away.

They struggled together in the crowd: Snick flicking his tongue repulsively in and out between his thin lips as if he were enjoying himself, Edward trying to keep his balance, trying not to look at the boy's cold eyes so close to his.

People surged on relentlessly round them. He was dimly aware that Helga and Wolf had been carried on by the crowd and were no longer a threat, but he concentrated on hanging on to the branch. Snick's grip was far stronger than Edward would have expected for someone so skinny, and his staring eyes were making him feel odd.

'Help me! Please help!' he begged the walkers that passed him, but no eyes flicked in his direction.

A new group was surging in from a side street to join the crowd on the Parade. A large, beefy man in a camel-hair dressing-gown drove between Edward and Snick. He banged up against the branch and slapped it out of his way with one careless, hefty hand, turning like a tank to go the same way as the rest of the crowd. With a hiss of rage Snick was knocked to one side; Edward, heavier though shorter, managed to keep his balance and his hold on the branch.

Snick's fingers loosened. With a sick feeling, Edward saw him fall gently backwards beneath the walkers, as if into a sinking sand. Immediately, the crowd closed over him as if he had never been there, and there was nothing Edward could do.

Snick is Locke's son, he reminded himself. *He'll survive to threaten someone else.*

They were coming to the end of the Parade. In the thick of the crowd Edward was carried past the last hotel, the public toilets, the car park; until the cottages had dwindled away behind them and they were out on the stony track, with the broad, flat expanse of the marshes and the river on one side and the sea wall on the other.

It had stopped snowing, and above them the icy stars hung glittering in the deep, black dome of space. The moon was almost full, silvering the faces of the sleepwalkers, shining coldly in their dreaming eyes.

In a great curve they swept to the left, up the track that led to the top of the sea wall, their feet ringing on the frosty stones. Along the surface of the wall, wide and broad as a road, they marched; and with that vast, silent army of dreamers went Edward, clutching the branch against him, not knowing where the march was to end, until he saw the squat black shape like a tree stump in the distance at the end of the sea wall.

They were going to the tower.

CHAPTER TWENTY-ONE

In the Shadow of the Tower

There were already people waiting there, hundreds of people it seemed to Edward, perhaps the whole population of Uffenham, standing in rows on the sea wall, standing on the steps that led down to the beach and round the tower mound. There were even people down on the beach, in a huge, motionless semi-circle, their figures dark in the shadow of the tower that striped the shingle like a tree-trunk. They reminded him of an audience waiting for latecomers before the show can start.

Now his part of the crowd was joining the others, moving in an orderly way to where there was still some space among the concrete rocks on the mound and down on the moonlit shingle.

Still no one spoke; everyone waited.

Edward looked round desperately for Bur. He'd better check he wasn't here before going down to the river.

He began to walk between the ranks of people, feeling curiously embarrassed as he looked up into their sleeping, silvered faces. There were some faces he recognized: the girl from the baker's who sold him bread every morning, an old fisherman from the beach, the secretary of the sailing club, in his battered peaked cap; but no one flickered an eyelid as he passed.

There were too many people. Then, as he gave up in despair, a figure holding a flaming brand ran out from the crowd below; a smell of burning tainted the cold, clean air.

As the crowd moved back, Edward saw the driftwood heaped high in the shadow of the tower. The wood was damp and took time to catch; it gave out little light at first, only a spiral of dark smoke, then there were orange sparks between the black figures on the snow-covered shingle. Pale shapes hung limply from the top of the pile, as if from a washing-line. They stirred as hot air began to rise from the burning wood, and a sudden murmur ran round the motionless crowd. In the flickering light he saw something shifting on the shingle where the little waves rolled in edged with moonshine.

The hull of a small boat.

Had they found the rowing-boat? In a panic he pushed his way through to the beach steps, clutching the branch like a talisman. 'Let me through!' he begged the people standing in his way, but no one appeared to hear.

He pushed down to the shingle, and skirted round the outside of the crowd. As soon as he was close to the boat, he knew it was the one from the creek. Melting snow pooled among the broken floorboards and the hull had a hard mud shell. Who had brought it here? Who else knew Bur was leaving at dawn?

The crowd had turned: row upon row of pale faces was watching him. Locke's children would be among them somewhere. Edward clutched the branch and darted for the shadow of the tower.

Close to, the shapes hanging from the sullen fire were recognizable. They were clothes that Bur had worn: the new pair of jeans, the T-shirt, a sort of night garment and Fen's towelling beach robe. The bottom of the jeans twisted in the hot air and flame jagged along one leg.

'Typical of the boy, standing about when he's a task to complete and very little time to do it!' snapped a familiar voice.

Edward saw Astrid, thin and grim in the firelight, her grey hair untidy and her eyes wild. She, and little Mae beside her, had materialized out of the dark crowd in the strange way they always did. There was no sign of Zelma, but he had a feeling she wouldn't be far away.

'Thank goodness!' he said. 'I thought you'd left. Can you tell me what's happening?'

'Nothing is, at the moment,' retorted Astrid. 'It's waiting for you.'

'Come, Edward,' said Mae softly. Her old eyes shone in the firelight as if they were still full of tears. 'You must make *Ringhorn* ready for Bur. You haven't long. Locke and his children are on their way.'

So they weren't here yet. 'But where's Bur?'

'He's coming. Meanwhile, *Ringhorn* must be made whole for the last voyage.' They were looking at him and waiting.

Edward gulped. 'You mean I've got to do it myself? Without Bur?'

'You've got the branch, dearie. That's all you need.' Mae patted his arm. 'It's time for Bur to go home to his island. Look . . .' She gestured at the dreaming faces about them. 'They're waiting for the ceremony. They've lit the fire, burned the clothes. It's the custom where Bur comes from, and they do it to honour him. Now, come, child. You know what to do with the branch.'

She gave him a gentle push. Reluctantly, he left the shadows and went over the shingle to where the hulk of the boat lay under the moon, small and insignificant in the breaking waves. The people were still watching him; he could see the whites of their eyes.

He bent forward. There was a tingling in his cold

hands as the branch slid in, and he let go in surprise. At once the air around him began to tremble, raising eddies of little stones and sand and spray, so that he had to shut his eyes. When he half opened them, the rowing-boat had disappeared. Something else was growing, expanding, becoming more solid, although he couldn't touch or see it. There was pressure on his face, a weight of air against his body. He felt his hair lift and a whirlpool spin round him, pulling at his cheeks and hands, sucking him into the creation of *Ringhorn*.

He wrenched himself back until he was safely with Mae and Astrid on the edge of the crowd. The sea was behaving normally again and the sand and stones had settled. He had the sensation of something tall and solid and powerful just metres away from him, yet, frustratingly, he seemed to see even less of it now than he had done on the marshes yesterday. What could the people see with their dreaming eyes that he could not?

'Is she there?'

'She's there,' Mae said.

As she spoke Edward felt a commotion behind him, then Mae's restraining hand on his arm. The crowd was stirring, moving back, parting like a wave, and there were dark figures at the top of the beach steps against the white of the tower mound where the thin snow lay.

One of the figures must be Bur. He wanted to run to them, but Mae's grasp was strong. With a shock he realized Astrid was holding his other arm. He twisted round and saw their faces.

In that terrible moment he knew.

They let him go at last, and he ran to where Bur was being carried down the beach to the fire. He saw who carried him: Locke, his face ruddy with triumph in the firelight, and his two sons, Wolf and Snick. Helga followed, her thin lips parted in a smile, black hair and black coat streaming out behind her. They cast Bur in his cloak down by the fire as if he were a bundle of old clothes and stood over him: four carrion crows, dressed in mock-mourning. Locke was in the city suit he had worn at the beginning, in his hand the mistletoe dart, from the deadly game.

Bur's fur-lined hood fell back and Edward saw that his eyes were open.

He's not going to die! he thought, in fierce joy. *Locke hasn't killed him, after all!* He thrust between Helga and Wolf, and fell on to the shingle beside him. 'What's he done to you?'

Bur's face was twisted with pain, but his eyes saw everything Edward felt, and were filled with pity. 'It was meant to be.'

'You won't die! I shan't let you!' Edward let go the hand he had been gripping and stood up. The people had encircled the group by the fire, their faces impassive.

'Is there a doctor here?' His shout seemed tiny, swallowed by the stars. But the people must have heard him! Still, it seemed, they slept, for not one of them moved to Bur's rescue.

'It's no good,' said Locke, his voice filled with hateful amusement. 'They know Bur is dying.'

'Then you're his murderer!' cried Edward.

'We each have our role in this story,' said Locke, shrugging. 'I've vanquished him, yes. But then it's always been a struggle for supremacy between us. I've played my role rather more successfully than he has, that's all.' He held out the mistletoe dart and looked at it thoughtfully before dropping it on the stones.

'It's never going to harm anyone else!' In bitter rage Edward caught the dart up by its unsharpened end. He pushed furiously through the unresisting crowd to the sea. With all his strength he hurled the dart away from him, far into the night. There was a distant splash.

Locke made no move to stop him. He was still standing by Bur's prone body as Edward came back to the fire. 'That thing's indestructible,' he said softly. 'One day a green stone will be washed up on a distant shore.' His three children sniggered as if he had said something witty.

In despair Edward looked at Bur's closed eyes. He pulled Bur against him, supporting his head. Bur's eyes opened and he managed a smile. 'Thank you for the shoes. It's time to take them back.'

He was still wearing Dad's old canvas beach shoes. As Edward eased them off, Bur sighed and something deathly crackled in the sigh. His bare feet looked bloodless and fragile; his huge frame seemed to have shrunk.

'Leave him.' Locke's voice was impatient. 'There's nothing you can do.'

Crouching by Bur, Edward stared around in anguish. The Newnes sisters had vanished but he could pick out other people he knew: Lyddie, not far off; Matt, with Vali by his side, their expressionless faces gilded by the fire. Beyond them was the thin figure of his uncle holding a bundle of fishing gear.

A movement at the edge of the crowd caught Edward's eye. For a moment he thought he saw a man in an old straw hat, someone who did not belong to Uffenham at all, until the figure melted into shadow. But now he remembered what Bur's father had said when he gave him the message.

It will save him in the end.

And he still had the message, didn't he? He'd never managed to give it to Bur. Carefully, Edward lowered Bur to the shingle and felt in the right-hand pocket of his jacket. There was only a small, rigid object, a shape he recognized: the front door key. Nothing else.

But in the other pocket was a curl of paper.

'Bur, look,' he whispered. 'Read this. It's from your father.' But Bur's eyes were glazed; he could see nothing.

In desperation Edward stood up and faced Locke. 'You're wrong. There is something I can do. I've a message from his father that will save him.' He held the scrap of paper out. 'It's the word.'

For a second Locke looked shaken. Then his smile was back. 'Then read it, Edward, read it.' He glanced about at the silent crowd and back at Edward, and his smile grew.

'Tell us all what the word is – if you can.'

CHAPTER TWENTY-TWO

The Word

The word was just as impossible to read as ever, especially by firelight. Edward had never been able to puzzle it out in daylight; he couldn't do so now. He stared and stared at the word, trying to keep his hand holding the paper from shaking, and all the while at his feet he could hear Bur taking hoarse, gasping breaths that were frightening to hear.

'Come on, Pa. Can't we get him moving?'

Wolf was restless, prowling round the fire, his teeth chewing on his bottom lip. He aimed an impatient kick at Bur's back.

'Stop that!' said Locke sharply. 'Let him die with dignity. Remember who he is.'

'It'll be daylight soon,' complained Snick, his white face glistening with the heat of the fire. 'We'll run out of time.'

Helga nodded her head in Edward's direction. 'He's

no threat, Pa. The word's a foreign language to him!' She looked greedily at Bur's dying body and licked her lips. 'You've beaten him this time, Pa. What a victory we shall celebrate, eh? The four of us shall rule the world!'

'My sweet creature of darkness,' Locke crooned, stroking her hair as if he gentled a wild beast, not a girl at all. 'You remember your task?'

She tossed her head and her dark mane flew. 'Of course.'

Locke flung his arms wide and his face was exultant. 'Then to it, my children!'

Edward was pushed aside. His father's shoes were kicked into the fire, and Bur's crumpled body scooped up by Wolf and Snick. Helga pranced round them, uttering high, inhuman cries that made Edward's scalp prickle. The crowd moved apart to let them carry their burden to the edge of the sea, and a desolate keening went through them as if they sensed that Bur's death was imminent.

'Wait! I've still got the word!' cried Edward, beating at Wolf's arms. Wolf snarled at him and did not let go.

Bur's head was lolling over Wolf's shoulder, his fair hair rumpled on the leather jacket. He opened his eyes at Edward's cry, and this time they focussed. Edward caught his whisper. 'Don't grieve for me. I have to die so that the Story can go on.

252

There is no end ever, for anyone; only a new beginning.'

Edward tried to push through after him, but the crowd was in his way. The next moment he had collided with someone he knew. Vali was looking down at him. A tiny flicker of recognition showed in her eyes, as if the bump had awoken her senses a little.

'Vali? It's me, Edward!' He shook her arm. 'Vali, you're dreaming, but in your dream you can see me, can't you?'

Her mouth opened as if she were in shock. She knew him, he was sure. He flashed the scrap of paper in front of her eyes. 'Can you see this, Vali?' Her eyes moved, following the paper in the air. 'You must help me, Vali! Can you read this word in your dream? It's not English. Do you know it?'

He held the paper so that the firelight shone on it. For a terrible moment he thought she would say nothing. Then her perfect lips parted. A word came out with complete clarity.

It was a word he had never heard before.

But as the word fell into the dying night, the crowd stopped their keening and stood still beneath the fading stars. In the grey dawn light they began to whisper it, turning to each other as if they were passing it on like a party game. After a moment's astonishment Edward stopped watching them. All he wanted to know was whether, like a magic spell, it had saved Bur.

He ran out from the crowd to the edge of the sea. Something dark and solid yet still invisible to him was being dragged into the waves under the lightening sky. He could hear stones grate beneath its hull. All he could see was the huge, black, leaping mare that pulled it and the yoke that bound her. Locke and his two sons stood by the water's edge, watching. There was no sign of Bur.

'Where is he?' cried Edward. 'What have you done with him?'

He knew that Bur had died and that they had put his body in the boat. He had died while Edward had been waiting for Vali to read the word. He'd waited too long: she'd read it too late.

He stood there alone on the shingle with the whispering crowd at his back. Tears shot from his eyes and burnt his cold cheeks; he couldn't stop them coming. He wept for Bur and for all the sadness he had kept inside since his father's death. And the sadness came out of its frozen, secret place and melted.

The crowd's whispering was growing louder. It chanted the word over and over again with increasing intensity. It reached Edward where he stood weeping; it made Locke and his sons turn and cover their ears.

As the word rose to a shout there was a sudden

dreadful shrieking from the mare; the water threshed with her panicking hooves. Edward looked up and through the shimmer of his tears thought he saw something coil from Locke's side into the water: a scaly tail flashed in the grey dawn light and was gone in a welter of dark bubbles.

Locke was holding back a huge wolf that snarled furiously at the crowd. He kept a restraining hand on its brindled fur as it growled and slathered; the other he held up for silence. His face was suffused with anger as he looked around, but even in that moment his voice was controlled.

'All right. You have your victory. You win. This time.'

Edward, bewildered, watched him wade into the water, seize the yoke that bound the screaming mare and loosen it, throwing himself on to her back. Together, horse and man broke free of the sea, sending cascades of foaming water down the mare's withers. The beach seemed to rock with the fury of their going. Stones shot like bullets from under the mare's hooves as they galloped away from the tower's shadow, down the shingle spit to where the land ended; and behind them streaked a wolf with fire in its jaws.

There was light and it wasn't from the fire.

There was something in the water: an arching rainbow of light against the sky. It wasn't the stars;

the stars had gone with the coming of the dawn. The sun was rising behind the horizon, and over the golden water there was the outline of a ship. And behind Edward the crowd had started up again: one word, repeated over and over again by hundreds of voices.

He saw the ship float out slowly over the waves, its burden dark within it. He saw a sail billow and fill with light and air; a horned prow that fanned the water into ripples of pink and palest gold. The sun was laying down a shining path for the ship to follow, and now the word was a jubilant cry from the crowd and although it was still in a language he did not know, he could at last understand it.

'Rebirth!'

The three Newnes sisters stood side by side. 'Look!' said Zelma, and her voice was strong. The light had washed the wrinkles from her cheeks so that she looked young and carefree. All three might have been girls, their hair gilded by the rising sun. Mae pointed over the water and her words rang out. 'He's going to his island!'

The huddled figure in the ship was stirring, rising to its feet, stretching out its arms on either side for balance as the ship sailed away into the bright disc on the horizon. The ship and the figure with outstretched arms sailed on, growing smaller and smaller until at last Edward was too dazzled to see the moment they merged with the sun.

He thought he heard Zelma whisper, 'Now do you understand, Edward?'

He took a deep breath. 'Does that mean—?'

The question was too big to put into words, and no one answered it.

He turned and the world was filled with light and warmth, but there was no one there. All that was left were the cold, dead embers of a beach fire that anyone might have lit. He knew it was over; but in a way it had only just begun: for himself and Dad, for Bur.

He walked over to the fire, and under his feet the stones shone like jewels. There were two objects lying in the ashes. He picked them up: they were his father's shoes, and they were unscorched.

Someone was crunching over the shingle towards him. It was Fen, a coat thrown over her men's pyjamas, her hair uncombed, her brisk edges rubbed away by sleep.

She thrust a plastic bag at him. 'You lot! You've left your breakfast behind.' She took him in properly, saw the shoes but didn't comment on them. Instead she gave a huge yawn and rubbed her eyes. 'I've had such dreams! Wonderful morning. I thought you'd be with Matt and Hodder. Aren't you going fishing with them?' She pointed up the beach where in the distance two figures were walking.

'Oh, yes. Yes, I am.' He took the bag, smiling at her.

'And I've got good news. Your mum rang last night. She's coming up for a few days.'

In sudden joy he flung his arms out, shoes in one hand, bag in the other, to the sun. 'Really?'

'Really.' She looked at him thoughtfully. 'It takes courage, doesn't it?'

Once she had disappeared back up the steps, he went over to the sea. He put the bag down on the shingle and leaned forward over the water, carefully putting the shoes in the tide's reach. It was going out, leaving a smooth band of clean, new sand where he stood. The waves lapped round the shoes as if to test them, then drew them down the sand.

'Take them for Dad,' he said softly. 'Wherever he is.'

Then he grabbed the bag and went racing, leaping, over the shingle into the new morning, after the two distant figures.

'Wait for me!' he shouted. 'I'm coming, too!'

When he looked back, the sea was smooth under a radiant sky. There was no sign of the shoes.

Author's Note

The other story woven in with Edward's is one of the most beautiful and powerful of the Norse myths, The Death of Baldur. Myths are living things, a way of expressing eternal truths through stories. This myth tells us that rebirth and regeneration are part of the endless cycle of nature.

Baldur is the beloved son of Odin, chief of the gods of the Aesir, and nicknamed the Shining One because he is so gentle and compassionate. But Baldur has been having terrible dreams that foretell his own death. Though Odin knows Baldur's death is fated, he desperately wants to prevent it.

Baldur's mother, Frigga, makes everything in creation swear not to harm him. She doesn't bother with the little mistletoe plant, which seems too weak to be dangerous. The gods invent a game to check everything is keeping the oath. In turn they hurl objects at Baldur – small ones like twigs and little stones at first, then bigger ones. When even Thor's hammer bounces off Baldur harmlessly, they laugh with relief. But alone among the gods, Loki, Odin's foster-brother, has always hated Baldur. When he discovers that the mistletoe plant hasn't taken the oath, he begins to plot Baldur's death.

The rest of the story happens as Edward himself sees it when he is taken into mythic time by the Newnes sisters (the Norns, who live beneath the great ash tree, Yggdrasill, and are the goddesses of destiny). Loki makes a dart from the mistletoe and guides blind Hodur, Baldur's own brother, in the throwing of it. The sharp end pierces Baldur and he dies.

Baldur's death is the beginning of Ragnorok, the end of creation, when Loki and his three monstrous children – the Fenrir Wolf, Hel and the Midgard Serpent – battle against the gods. But after fire and flood, Baldur and his brother Hodur return from the dead, and a new world is born.

The End will be the Beginning.

MURKMERE

Patricia Elliott

'Yours is an unblemished soul, Aggie,' he whispered, 'a sweet, pure delicacy of a soul – and we must keep it that way, mustn't we?'

Born and brought up in a small village, Aggie knows that she must never question the power of the divine beings – the birds – nor the omens in the Table of Significance. But when the Master of Murkmere Hall summons her to be companion to his ward, Leah, she enters a new and disturbing world. Leah is headstrong, spoilt and unhappy, and challenges everything Aggie has ever known to be true.

Secrets and betrayals lurk within the old house, and when the shadowy but all-powerful Ministration arrive for a grand ball, questioning becomes a dangerous game . . .

Jan Mark says of Murkmere: *'Patricia Elliott has created and sustained a wonderfully foreboding atmosphere where nature and man are united in decay and superstition.'*

AMBERGATE

Patricia Elliott

'I am the girl with no name . . . I have a secret I must never tell. If I do, they will come after me – the Protector and his men.'

Only a number branded on her arm betrays the orphan girl's past. When she arrives at Murkmere Hall to be a kitchen maid, they call her Scuff; little do they guess that she has committed a terrible crime. Haunted by her dark secret, all Scuff can do is pray to the divine beings – the birds – for forgiveness.

Now, five years later, the past is catching up with Scuff. Hunted from all sides, she flees Murkmere, only to be forced back to the cruel confines of the Capital, and the Orphans' Home where it all began.